THE GATES OF
PARADISE

To Peter,
My dear, dear
brother, with lots
of love,

BOOKS BY GWYNETH CRAVENS

The Black Death
(with John S. Marr)
Speed of Light
Love and Work
Heart's Desire
The Gates of Paradise

THE GATES OF
PARADISE

Gwyneth Cravens

TICKNOR & FIELDS

New York 1990

For information about permission to reproduce selections
from this book, write to Permissions, Ticknor & Fields,
215 Park Avenue South, New York, New York 10003.

Library of Congress Cataloging-in-Publication Data

Cravens, Gwyneth.
The gates of paradise / Gwyneth Cravens.
p.   cm.
ISBN 0-89919-981-X
I. Title.
PS3553.R278G38   1990   90-42550
813'.54—dc20   CIP

Printed in the United States of America

BP 10 9 8 7 6 5 4 3 2 1

The poem "Estigio" by David Rosenmann-Taub
is used by permission of the poet.

To Luc Brébion

Estigio

Patinir.

Fuego de la verdad,
Caronte,
ya te vi.
No me mires *a mí*.
Mira, por caridad,
el horizonte.

David Rosenmann-Taub

One

NOTHING of the dream remained. He removed his satin sleep mask — a piece of the night — and reached for his water glass. A cool sip. Perhaps he would drift back. . . . No, he was quite alert. Maybe he had some profound disorder that would prevent him from ever finishing his work. The doctor would ask, after hearing him out, "Insomnia?" The roof creaked, his wife stirred. His wife, his refuge, his help, his comfort. Next to him, closer than during the daylight hours, lay her slight form, warm and breathing and unconscious. His throat tightening, he carefully rested his hand on her arm.

His woman and his house. He was safe. But still he couldn't sleep. What about his work? He had the evidence, the documentation of his spectacular find —

You'll never do it, you'll never begin, said the voice (his own).

He was really awake now. Without question. If only he

exercised more, as on those summer days when he had biked, gardened, walked on the beach, plunged into the bay. A sensation of floating and sinking on the swells all night long. But tonight he was as stiff as a plank. His knee bothered him. His jaw. No more dental work, please. . . . His wife said insomnia was caused by unresolved hostility. If he turned on the light to read, it would rouse her, and naturally she wouldn't be pleased, although if a phone call awakened her instead, she would be attentive, clear-voiced, and gracious. And if it were an emergency, she would respond swiftly, with forceful, murmured counsel, as she reached for her clothing. Certain that if anything terrible ever befell him she would take care of him, fight for him, he would watch her dash down the hall into the darkness.

Well, insomnia was no emergency. . . . How long had he been lying here? The wall of black was pierced by a vertical bar, an opening in the curtains; radiance diffused through the misty sky from a low orange moon that only a few hours ago had hung in the opposite window. The circuit was almost complete. Down the hall his parents might still be snoring in their room, and he could call to Mama for help. (Just close your eyes, dear, and think of something very beautiful, she would murmur, putting her hand on his forehead.) No, everything was turned around now: he lay awake in his parents' room. His mother was far away. Maybe he had become an old, old man now, addled, and his whole life had passed in the space of a day. . . . Think about the things you have to do tomorrow, the work you're too afraid to begin, the women you have desired — that was scarcely restful.

He went downstairs, poured milk into a pan on the stove,

and turned on the television to a program about Gothic cathedrals. The stove clock read 3:42 A.M. On the floor of Chartres before the altar was a mysterious spiral maze. If only he could visit cathedrals with a camera crew instead of having to think about Mauritius, and who was interested in a seventeenth-century Dutch painter, anyway?

The pan boiled over. He poured what remained into a cup and sat down in the sun-room and opened the *Symposium*. The smoothness of the creamy pages, the square weight on his lap, invited him to step into the book, to leave behind his own location and thoughts, to listen to the speech of the wise woman Diotima: "But what if man had eyes to see the true beauty — the divine beauty, I mean, pure and clear and unalloyed, not clogged with the pollutions of mortality and all the colors and vanities of human life — thither looking, and holding converse with the true beauty simple and divine?" And what were the pollutions of mortality? All knowledge was immediately available — you needed only to look. His wife liked to say that, and it was true.

His skin was cooling, his body growing heavier. Perhaps he might slowly wake her up, and put his hand on her breast, and kiss her ear. But she might not welcome an invasion — what trust she had in him to sleep next to him night after night! Closing his eyes, he saw amber rays passing through lace; it was like the girl's fichu as she stood holding the open book before the candlelight in Mauritius's *The Instruction of the Virgin*.

He started up the stairs. Suddenly the birds began. First one, and then another, and another and another, and then a whole racket, much louder and more insistent than any bird racket sent up during the day. He peered out the little window in the stairwell. The sky was white; the trees of the hedgerow stood up black against the mist. In the garden, the silhouettes of the dwarf apple, with its flaring crown, and the dwarf pear, with its ogival crown, remained motionless. Only he was awake. Perfect! he thought. Here I am.

Sunlight flashed off the bay, passed through the boughs of the cedar and the part in the curtains, and struck the mirror. (The mirrors and windows in the house conspired: *There is no world but ours.*) The mirror distilled the light and shot it down the dark stairwell, painting a grove of wavy filaments on the wall.

She tosses on the pillow, the mirror told the chest of drawers, the corner cupboard, and the chair, all of them rising and falling, gently ballooning into the room. *Side by side they lie under the blue patchwork. Toes, lips, twitch.*

His flesh grew effervescent, and a gentle pull, no more than that of gravity on light, lifted him up and over low hills until he came to a town, a square, and a building with room after room of paintings. He entered a Botticelli and descended into an aromatic glade. As he floated over a mosaic of herbs and flowers, his soles brushed spongy moss, and every detail sprang to his eye at once: each leaf vein, the pollen dust on each petal. Back in a gallery with a polished floor and a high ceiling, he searched for another painting to enter. Most were false doors, nothing but thin coats of pigment on unyielding surfaces. But here — here was something! With pleasure, he passed through a thick blue-green gel into a Canaletto and swam in flickering, ridged waters. In a dim room, lit up by a hazy golden shaft, a girl stepped out of her bath, glancing over her shoulder; she had just been staring at something that left its luminous trace in her eyes as she turned her head. Her mouth was slightly open, her gaze compelling. He — all of a piece, pure music, singular, the result of a million years of elaboration — found himself surging toward her. This was what he was made to do. His feet touched the polished floor again. And here *she* was. The years separating him from her compressed between them and vanished. Her thigh against his, her mouth on his, an unbearable erotic fusion. He twisted, and his elbow, suddenly present, grazed a solid form that shifted away from him.

New again, supine, he listened to his own breath in his nostrils. She was gone, replaced, as he opened his eyes, by a deep satin black, a barely perceptible shine, a film, perhaps a reflection of the membrane of the eye. Below the rim of the mask, daylight, a tangled, brown, leafless forest, a long, rounded, pink escarpment, and blue uplands in shadow. A bird-cry tumbled through the smell of the sea. Branches swept against shingles. The forest moved.

She turns her head. He twists, stretching an elbow. Skin awakened, he extends his foot and sighs. In the room out there, in the room in here, they stir in their black masks. They are entering the day's long corridor of sensations.

She remained a warm sliver under her sleep mask. Today — today! She had no age and no memory of who she was supposed to be. She pushed the mask up.

The pieces of furniture withdrew to their daytime postures and became solid, with soft shadows blurring their edges. She had been admiring herself, her lovely dress, in a mirror until a movement at her back startled her, and she had glimpsed the old, terrifying beast-head just before she was sucked underneath the weight of the ocean. Otherwise, the content of the night, its story, had dissolved, leaving her with the sense that the truth was in one room and she was in another, uneasy, looking around, looking over her shoulder. Where's the thing I'm searching for? Not here, not in this room. This room was not enough. She felt like waving her fists in the air and crying.

But the smiling puckers of the quilt binding announced that the world was wonderful and that she was a success. I'm happy — she threw off her mask — I wake up happy, one of my best characteristics. I'm happy because today — How wonderful, that moment when he gazes at you and wants you, wants you so much that he drops the mask of suavity and control, and he's prepared to risk everything to be with you, and you're enjoying his regard, perhaps a little aroused, but not yet sure what you'll decide about him. You come into the room, and he's tugged to his feet by the simple act of your entrance. There you are, smiling, laughing perhaps, even on the arm of someone else, and your whole body, made beautiful and alert by his attention, senses him as if he were under your breastbone, and you're aware that he's following you, and you know you are not the slave of your emotions, ah, no, you control all the atoms in the room, all the atoms in the universe. That moment, rounded, crystalline, contains all the possibilities of an un-ruined future, of immortality.

I am happy — she said to herself, and felt the purity of the sensation, a straight line passing through her heart —

because I know what I want and I'm going to get it. She examined her mottled palms, still indented with little crescents from her nails. (She observed herself; yes, she was conscious; this was the proof; she was not frightened by a beast-face in the glass, she was not gasping at the bottom of the sea.) These hands had been held and kissed and soon would be again. He knew her completely, as no one else ever had. Just to smell his skin made her mad with joy. (She heard herself announcing this fact to herself.) She drew in a deep breath and settled the quilt around her shoulders, destroying the hills and rearranging the shadowed valleys. God — her God, as clear as the day, as present as air — let me be receptive to you, let me escape chaos, let me do everything today in sacred perfection.

More strokes of light entered, kindling a fire in the mirror, bringing alive a swarm of dust grains over the bed, revealing on the sill, not a foot from her eye, a dead fly and a single blond hair. Why wasn't this place clean? Something had to be done. She loved order; she loved the peace it brought; she was delighted by a neat row of polished, transparent jars or a succession of hours lived calmly, fully, and with attention. She wanted to be impeccable; she did not want to offend God. But she had no time. Dust particles slowly fell; windows acquired streaks; insect wings collected on ledges; cracks widened in beams. Cartilage hardened; droplets of fat accumulated in organs; blood vessels constricted; bones flaked away; vision dimmed and hearing grew muffled; flesh sagged.

And why, why couldn't she remain cradled in a single prolonged kiss? Why couldn't she be permitted to inhabit a place without dust or wrinkles? She longed to rest in the empty, fan-shaped, blue chamber constructed by the gaze of love. In this room, unalloyed and constant passion flowed out of her, out of — out of her lover; they were immersed in it as if in a bath of some highly refined, gleaming substance. But she had awakened in exile, a room away from the truth, in a space cluttered with objects — a big bed, a slumbering form (oh, him; there was the nape of his neck with its boyish curve), a chest of drawers, a mirror, a cupboard. Tree silhouettes undulated on the curtain. The little black clock ticked, its red hand restlessly shifting. Her right side, nearest him, was warmer than her left. She turned her hip. Yes, she inhabited this body and no other; she could keep the wrong things from happening, find a solution to any problem. Every day it was important to decide precisely what to do from beginning to end. Control her flaws. Avoid the mire of distraction. In the drawer waited the letter, the ring, the shell. She would live the day beautifully, in complete consciousness.

She placed her hand on her husband's chest. She needed to compose her Sunday talk (on what? she had to come up with something soon; love, passion, *agape?*), and she had appointments, and she had to return phone calls — about hospital visits, about whether children should be allowed to carry candles in the meetinghouse for the Harvest Festival, about buying a bigger coffee urn for the table for the homeless at the bus terminal, about the placement of the poor box in the meetinghouse parking lot, about a petition protesting the imprisonment of innocents in Central America, about disease, craziness, old age, and death. . . .

But if she could be sure of him; if this time at last she could really be sure — perhaps she could consider making time to see him, changing her schedule. A pity she couldn't afford a secretary! But why pay someone to do what she herself could do better? Anyway, she didn't want people poking around in her private business, and it made more sense for her to keep that money. Besides, there were always volunteers. On her lunch hour she would not eat; she would will herself to be thin. She would drive into town and buy the ivory dress. But first of all, there was the project of making her husband obliviously content.

The oval of warmth over his heart caused him to remove the mask. The brain, dim and remote, receives the light and all its tricks. The eye sees upside down, but the brain believes this: that a room exists, with webs and daubs of gold here and there and that someone it considers "I" lies stretched out, part of the body still one with the bed and the flat, easy plateau of sleep. The blue uplands heaved under the forest of her hair. "O world, thou was the forest to this hart." Was that how it went? And she — was it she? — was the heart to thee. The world to thee? Her skin in the steadily paling shadow was the skin of a Leonardo Madonna, a coalescence of soft hues lit as if from within. He drew in her scent — of leaves, of some spicy wood, of the tide — and tasted it.

If only he could stay hidden here, next to her! He could ask her about the quote — she was always quoting things — but then she might jump up and run downstairs to her study and lug the heavy volume of Shakespeare onto the bed. He must make himself remember: he had entered paintings; he had recaptured passion, purpose. Today, he must do something astonishing. But how to begin — to find a way inside? If only he did not remember what he had once been, what good fortune others enjoyed, what that old passion had been. Or if only he were like the man in Russia who could recollect every single thing, every detail, and so could not recognize a familiar face day after day because it had subtly changed.

Melpomene put her arms around James, pressing her mouth against his neck, still hot and damp from deep sleep, and looked up into his eyes. They were heavy-lidded, nearsighted, and mildly surprised, like a newborn's. He blinked twice, as if to ask, comically, Well, who are you? She pushed her leg against his and kissed his ear, his eye. So simple, bringing him to her, and for the rest of his life, she was quite confident, he was hers. She watched her hand stroking his chest (the dress had a V neck, a pleated bodice that flattered her breasts, and the skirt hung in soft folds; perhaps, if she decided to see him, she would wear the red-gold ring; she would come down a curving stairway and . . .), swirling her fingers on his abdomen. "What do you want today, dear?" she murmured, so low that he thought for a second it was a breeze in the branches outside the window.

He gave her a squeeze and sat up, making the bed frame creak. Smiling and squinting, he felt around on the night table for his glasses. "That's quite a question! I'll have to think." He had to remain clear: he must begin, because if he did not begin, he would forget, and he would be surpassed, obliterated, and the way to remember was, O world thou was the something — or did the dream come before that? His wife had taught him the importance of an organized day. Discipline. He would analyze the slides, the documents. Make notes. Use his intelligence. Tonight, after dinner — it embarrassed him to ask her this now, outright — he would take her hand and lead her up the stairs; no, he would pick her up, he would carry her the way he had the first time he had brought her here, and he would place her across the bed. All of today the pleasurable tensions of anticipation would accompany him; she would reward him with her delicate kisses, her hands finding exactly the right places. She was splendid! How could he even think of some old love? Well, he wasn't responsible for his dreams. He settled the cold glasses on his nose. The room straightened: edges became distinct; lozenges of light on the floor became hard. "Hello, darling," he said.

Had he rejected her? Was it so? He who always responded promptly to the slightest brush of her fingertip?

He curved his spine so it cracked, and he yawned. "I had an amazing idea about my work, in the night. But I don't want to talk about it just yet."

"No — keep it to yourself. You know I never pry." Of course: he ought simply to shout it at her. His desire had disappeared, and his love. Burning, she would conceal her hurt. Flee. "Oh, look at the time! And I have so much to do."

He put his bare soles on the floor. Was she reproaching him for his idleness? For his failures? For the successes of everyone else? No, of course she was not reproaching him — she had just caressed him and asked what he wanted. The floorboards came into being under him. Today he would work. Tonight, as his reward, make love to her. "I'm going to start the book today." Saying it aloud would make it happen. "But how about breakfast? Croissants, raspberries, cappuccino —"

Her lips parted and turned down. Her lack of appetite was

the result of her finely tuned nerves, as were her fears — of burglars, of electricity, of the dark, of sharp blades, of trucks on highways, of tidal waves. She thought of livestock snuffling at their troughs, snouts plunged into slop. But what a cruel image that was! "No, thanks. But you have yourself a lovely breakfast, dear."

He found his slippers. The floor had been there all night; it was he who had been absent, who had flown. He fell into a stare. How was it that every morning his body, his brain, performed the miracle? How was it that in an instant the laws of sleep were broken and he was knocked back inside time and space? An alien will had meanwhile kept the boards in place. Something to tell Melpomene, later, when she was in a more talkative mood. His knees and calves trembled for an instant as he stood. Every morning he remembered all over again how to walk. Incredible. Would he begin today? Really? Before he put his glasses on, when the world was a blur, and her hair was a forest, he had *known,* he had been compelled, as if by the same force that held matter together, to do something important. Now, the gloomy, faintly sour air of the bedroom, the sharp corners of the furniture, his wife scowling and rubbing her cheek — all said no.

Her cheek was wet. Tears? Yes. Just before she awoke, the fleeting beast-face, horrible; she had plunged under the deep water; cried. Yes, he had turned away from her, yawning, bored. "I'm very happy," she said aloud. "I'm very well."

"Oh, good, darling."

She watched him yank open the curtains. He paid no attention to how the sun made her wince. Or to what that wincing might mean about what lay in store for her head today (but maybe she would escape). No, thumb to his teeth, he shuffled like a baby toward the bathroom.

The bedside telephone rang, and she answered in a soft, musical voice.

"I'm just calling to say goodbye, and then I won't bother you again."

"Mother —"

"I'm feeble and alone and it's horrible, you'll see. I have no one — I don't want to live."

"What happened?" These calls were becoming more frequent. Melpomene got up and pulled the quilt taut. "Did something happen?"

"No, nothing, nothing ever happens. I'm just going to say goodbye, and that will be that. My new will is on the desk."

"Please — it grieves me when you talk like that. Please, dear. I know it's difficult, I understand, I know, I know. I'll come right away, and we'll go out for dinner, and we'll have a nice walk, and you'll see how happy you'll be. And just think of all the nice friends you have, and a daughter who loves you, and a maid who adores you, and you have a beautiful apartment — just look out the window. Isn't it sunny there, too? Nice, warm — it's going to be a wonderful day. What more could you want? Think of all the poor people on the street who have nothing."

"You'll come?"

"Of course!" She plumped up the pillows, six of them, with flounces threaded through with ribbon. "I'll have to make some special arrangements. You know my schedule."

"And you'll stay a long time, not just for one of your half-hour house calls?"

"We'll go for a walk, we'll look at your garden, I'll take you to dinner —"

"I miss you, Mellie. Everything changes when you're here. You know, I've been rereading your father's sermons, and there's one that begins with the story of how you recited that whole passage about the over-soul at that dinner party when you were nine. After that, everyone in the fellowship wanted to know my child-rearing methods."

" 'Our faith comes in moments; our vice is habitual,' " intoned Melpomene, pleased and yet self-mocking. " 'Yet there is a depth in those brief moments which constrains us to ascribe more reality to them than to all other experiences.' That passage?"

"Oh, I don't know. I hate Emerson. He never would have written that if he had to put up with what I do."

"Mother, you need to get up and move around, go out and do some shopping. A new dress! How about that?"

After saying goodbye, Melpomene took a deep breath and put on her glasses. She hated them; they made her look pinched and grave, like the smartest, least-dated girl she had been in boarding school. No matter. She would have her contact lenses in before anyone saw her. She peered through the warped glass out at the lawn, the line of yellowing trees, the field, the marsh, the bay. She took Kuno's letter from the dresser drawer. Today his call might come. The power to decide was hers. How insolent of her mother to say that about Emerson! Over the field a hawk was circling. She could make out the separate feathers extended at the wing tips. She did not care. James cared, and, injured by his indifference, by his leap out of bed, she was not going to point the hawk out to him. But no — she had to wrench away from spite, immediately. "There's your hawk, dear," she sang out.

She slipped on her watch, with its black face and urgently blinking digits in their silver frame. The day had begun without her. The day would end without her. She had to hurry.

The house stood on a grassy rise among cedars, willows, and catalpas. Winds off the bay riffled through the shingles and in winter made the frame shudder. Even in summer a draft rose from under the stairwell, where there was no foundation but clay, in which arrowheads and broken pottery had been found by James's great-grandfather Aldrich. He had built the house at a time when sun and air were considered dangerous, and so mildew bloomed on the spines of the books that lined many of the narrow rooms. Webs clotted with flies hung in the corners of the living room, which was so dark and chilly that no one cared to enter it, and the wasps that mysteriously multiplied there crawled over the little warped panes and left their carcasses here and there.

No one had thought much about how to arrange the interior. James's grandmother had placed mirrors throughout the rooms, and his first wife had scattered around needlepoint cushions, now faded, and persuaded James to put up expensive canvases splashed with red and black over which the artist had pasted newspaper headlines about assassinations. When James fell in love with Melpomene, he brought in a carpenter to add on a sun-room, break open a wall of the kitchen, and install a bay window and a long pine table.

"This house is yours — do with it whatever you want," he had told her, even though his first wife had not yet moved out.

Melpomene replied with tears. She had sworn to herself when she decided to become a minister that she would dedicate her life to genuine service — not the subservience to the old-rich congregation that her father, out of snobbery, had practiced — and so she had been a wanderer on the face of the earth for years, fixing up rental apartments, rectories furnished with donations, ecumenical communes in slums, and shabby houses she or some fellowship or other had purchased in neighborhoods on the rise. She was moved by James's offer even more than by his love. Each of those places had, for a while, been designated her final, even ideal, home, the one in which she planned to grow old, but then some new opportunity would arise: acceptance at the seminary after she was seized by her vocation and quit medical school; the appearance of a poet who became her husband; ordination, such as it was in her freethinking, rather intellectual sect; an assignment to a church; divorce; reassignment; a new marriage, to an architect who had come to her with his wife for counselling (Melpomene had subsequently asked for a transfer); an increase in property values (she now had a small but prosperous portfolio); another divorce; another reassignment, this time, at her request, to a horrifyingly poor neighborhood; an offer of a lecturer's chair at a seminary; and finally, her successful campaign to take over the faltering, leaderless fellowship in the town near James's country house. When he led her from room to room one time when his wife was away and showed her views of the bay and the garden, Melpomene had exclaimed in a trembling voice, "This will be my last home; here I stay!"

Intending to transform the entire house, she, too, after their marriage, broke down walls, first turning the pantry and the rear screen porch into a study with an adjoining waiting room. The office resembled her previous ones: shelves of books; a tree-of-life carpet from the Caucasus which had been in her father's study at the rectory where she grew up; a comfortable leather chair for her and a low sofa and an end table and, in an ornate silver box, tissues for visitors; a stripped-pine writing table above which hung an antique mirror and framed photographs and mementos. On a pedestal stood a small plaster copy of the bust of an angel sculpted by Michelangelo which she had bought after admiring the original in a church in Rome years ago. Some of the more liberal members of her various fellowships, board members and the like, had been vexed by the piece. The sect didn't believe in angels; she had been forced to explain more than once, with considerable flair, that the angel, executed by one of the greatest of all humanists, simply represented the noblest qualities a human could ever hope to attain. When James informed her that the angel was not Michelangelo's, giving as evidence the long nose, which was out of proportion to the rest of the face, a mistake the artist would not have made even as a boy, she was annoyed, but then Kuno had agreed, and Kuno truly knew art. Now she wanted to get rid of this Pinocchio and to put in its place a copy of the real Michelangelo angel, to be found, James said, in the Casa Buonarroti in Florence (when would she ever be free to go there? Kuno might, with his uncanny intuition, divine her wish and bring one back).

Her zeal for renovation had continued, and she had converted the bedroom above her study into an office for James. No wonder he hadn't been able to work, crouched as he was in the dining room under the menace of the carved break-front, in the presence of the late-Victorian chairs, lined up like so many critics. He needed a bigger vision. Whenever she spoke of selling this furniture (ugly but worth a fortune), he flinched, thinking of his ancestors. He also reacted that way when she urged him to get rid of the modern art; he was still afraid of his first wife. Melpomene had made curing him of guilt and fear one of her chief projects. But lately she had so little time. Her plans for the living room, the master bedroom, the guest rooms, had been set aside for now.

This was their house, then: half changed, half neglected. Her study still smelled of paint. In closed-off rooms, plaster dust sifted down and skeins of lint attached themselves to the legs of unused beds. A blond hair from the head of James's first wife lay in a curl on a windowsill, her stiff linen hand towels hung untouched in the downstairs powder room. Grains of sand drifted into cracks between the floorboards. James and Melpomene went in and out the front door. Members of the fellowship seeking counsel came one by one or in couples to the outside entrance to her waiting room.

The mirrors leaned out from the paneling in high places; they caused windows to flash out of solid walls lined with looming armoires; they seduced the viewer into thinking he was seeing other rooms, other landscapes. The mirrors imitated the windows; the windows reflected the sky and the mirrors; mirrors contained windows, and windows contained mirrors. They caught and released Melpomene and James, who were scarcely aware of what it was that sheltered them from the wind, protected them from the sun and the frost, and remained present even when they slept.

T<small>WO</small>

T<small>HEIR</small> <small>BODIES</small> moved slowly. They washed. They forced limbs through sleeves and trouser legs. They thrust feet into shoes. Formerly difficult tasks performed without a thought. The labor required to master the operation of the washcloth in the convolutions of the ear, the passage of the comb through tangles, and the mechanics of the button and the shoelace was now forgotten, and so were the mornings when their fingers had been thick and slow, their nerves awkward, and a P and a B seemed identical, and the figures on the clockface were hieroglyphs.

Melpomene wore a bathrobe of emerald green cashmere. She owed herself just a few luxuries, then, like this robe as soft as moss, in the midst of her poverty, on the brink of her ruin (at any moment she could lose everything and suddenly find herself stranded). Today Kuno would return. To hear his voice once more — she asked for nothing else. Just when she had knocked down the walls, built new ones, painted them; just when she had succeeded in waking up without wanting to feel his mouth on hers; just when she was able again to tolerate the way she looked, the letters had begun to arrive.

Kuno had tracked her down in her new life. Intoxicated, she composed stunning replies; after all, he was an ocean away. No danger. She wrote of her deep satisfaction with her work and with James. She told him about her walks along the beach, the subtle hues of sky and bay and field which any painter would cherish, the garden, the simple dinners she prepared, the way the fellowship had begun to flourish, the rows of approving, upturned faces on Sunday mornings. But now Kuno was coming back. "I now see I'm nothing without you," he reported in his calligraphic handwriting. Could she forgive him? Perhaps that was the charitable thing to do — not to run away from him; he needed her.

James watched his wife bend over and pick out a pair of ballet slippers from the dozens of pairs of shoes in careful rows on racks in her closet. So dear, she was. A little girl. Her lovely curved bottom, her pelvis like a lyre, her light step. She was his! He could grasp her hips, lift her robe. . . . Ah, tonight.

He buttoned his shirt. Melpomene knew about all the others; he had told her his dreams; she had penetrated his deepest crevices. But she must never know about Alice, the erotic fusion, the only woman who — but what a useless train of thought. Years had passed. Anyway, he declared to himself, putting his chin up as if ready to take on all challengers, Melpomene is the only woman I have truly loved. She had honored him by choosing him; she fixed her solemn eyes on him and listened to secrets that he had never before thought he could utter. She took away his misgivings, his foolish timidities. She flew right to the most painful lesion and gave it her healing touch. Who cared if his name was no longer mentioned — out there? The point was that he evolve, that he do his absolute best. For the first time since his adolescence, under her influence, he had wanted to live the examined life, to be conscious of the play into which he had been born. Unlike anyone else he had ever met, Melpomene had a genuine calling, which was to understand herself and to inspire those around her to do the same; she had found a way to make her intuitions about religion harmonious with modern philosophy. Her ardor for change ignited in him ideas and aspirations at a time when he had felt bitter and depleted. During their courtship she would copy out quotations from Thoreau, Schopenhauer, St. Matthew, and the Song of Solomon and mail them to him. She interpreted these thinkers according to her dedication to the conscious life, of whom Christ was the representative. And she swore she would sustain him in his work. When he had returned from the ordeal of putting his mother in a home, Melpomene ran down the stairs, eyes bright. I have a surprise! A surprise for you! (She detested receiving surprises, as he had discovered after giving her a birthday party, but she loved to spring them.) She had embraced him hard, and even wept a little when they kissed, and she grabbed his hand and led him up the stairs and flung open the door to the bedroom that had been his as a child and more recently his mother's. "Now you can have complete privacy for your work. Now you can begin." As in "Aladdin and His Magic Lamp," when, in a single night, a jeweled palace had been constructed by a genie, she had crafted up an enchantment.

Even a box of his favorite bittersweet chocolates sat on the desk next to the new computer.

"We'll have a nice lunch," he said, pulling a sweatshirt over his head. From the darkness that smelled pleasingly of himself, he said, "Yesterday I went to the farmers' market."

She turned her head to look at him, her cheeks flushed, her shoulder blades fragile wings under her robe. "Oh, you don't have to fix anything on my account." What if today, during her visiting hours, Kuno were to appear? She put back the ballet slippers and chose a pair of custom-made pumps. It was he who had taught her about custom-made shoes.

James put his arms around her. "Darling," he told her hair, "I want to fix something for you — something you'll love."

"I'm running late." She removed his arms and opened a drawer and searched through her underclothes, through mounds of black and ecru and taupe lace and satin. But what was it? What was it? The sudden pressure in her head, in her chest, a kind of traveling aneurysm, urged her on. But why? Her skull remembered, and her hand, but not her brain; a slight tension ordered her to search. She watched her hands busily roving. Hunt, hunt! If you do not find it, death will find you. At any moment.

In the small bathroom down the hall, he picked up the horn-handled straight razor that had been his father's. No need to shave — he wouldn't be going anywhere today. But from the painting, the girl had beheld him; he wanted to make himself clean and smooth. Spreading foam over his cheeks, he began to cut away the accumulation of the night, the cells that had grown in the dark. He tightened his upper lip over his teeth; he turned his head and jutted his jaw. The razor, extremely sharp, made a faint rasp against his skin. She had been just as real as his face, now revealing itself, pink and fresh, with each swipe of the blade, and they had embraced on the floor of the gallery or museum or whatever it was, and he had received a boon, a shining pulse of energy.

Melpomene ran water in the sink in the big bathroom. She took off her glasses, and the world softened. The pressure transformed itself into pure joy. What she loved most was the astonishing beauty that God showered on the world — the fall leaves so tenuously clinging to the branches, the desire that contracted the iris of a man's eye, the passages of counterpoint in a complex fugue, the silence that held the fellowship together for a moment when everyone was simultaneously moved. Sometimes she thought: Stop, I can't take in one more impression! Every neuron would be firing. And yet she inevitably would see her hand reaching for the washcloth on its peg on yet another day, and that image would be stored in her brain for as long as she lived, added to the thousands of images of her hand reaching for the washcloth which already were laid up in her memory, useless, in rows of transparent jars. Every reach was exactly recorded: electrons aligned themselves in her brain to hold the image of her hand grasping the nubby maroon cloth. What was our eternity but this? That would make a good talk. What Is Our Eternity? After death you might not go to some other place. You might only wander in a field of harvested impressions. You might not even be able to choose which ones to relive. The bathroom mirror contained a flock of squawking crows and window mullions and, set in the flaming crown of an oak, a white-lit windowpane and her face. Yes, that's how it really was, if you paid attention. The Kingdom of the Father is spread upon the earth, and men do not see it. She needed to hurry. Her skin was lineless, firm against the wet cloth; her hair thick, dark, and glossy; no one ever guessed how old she was. Yes, you are lovely, a Georges de La Tour Magdalene! A girl in love in the morning. No beast-face behind her. The letter. She was loved. She would be saved. Today he would call, and if she forgave him. . . . Her lips formed an O. Her mouth, held this way, was bewitching; she constructed a kiss.

James stumped down the hall, whistling.

She quickly pulled away from the mirror. Had he seen her posing? She couldn't afford to be careless, even if he had no passion left. She had to maintain his love. After all, it was good for him, it sustained him; otherwise he would sink into utter self-absorption. And Kuno was scarcely reliable. "You're such a dear," she sang out. If she were to decide to go to Kuno, she would have to be skillful about James. She would harden herself to his slights. And of course she wanted to keep him in her life, too. Her love — she saw it as a bright cord — never broke. Her old lovers and husbands still wrote and called and sent her gifts. Some remained wonderfully desperate, even jealous. Until Kuno's last letter, she had thought he was the exception.

"You're so good." She ran to James, arms outstretched.

Puzzled, he grinned and closed his eyes and pressed his cheek against the top of her head. No one else had ever hugged him with such earnestness. Had something been bothering him? He forgot it. Had he been a little nervous about her earlier mood? No need. "You're the good one," he said. "I mean it."

"No, I really am not good at all," she said, brushing her lips along his throat.

"Oh," he breathed, "you *are* bad." Her touch, her voice, her presence like an elixir: he was awakened. How alive the air in the hallway here, and just look out the window at the flashing bay! What drama in the day ahead! He began to kiss her, but she drew away, which only enticed him.

"No time." She planted her hands on his chest and pushed. Laughing, he took a hasty step to keep his balance. "Incidentally, James, dearest, please don't let anyone see you in that sweatshirt."

"I'll play the hiding game when people come. Secret lovers, like old times." He went downstairs, humming.

She chose a violet angora sweater James had given her during the days when he used to sneak into the city for their trysts. The noise of the coffee grinder rose from below, together with some piano piece he had put on and his off-key accompaniment. *Bom, bom-pa-dum, bom, pah-dee-dah!* What a violet, like the horizon on a summer night; his awareness of color was enormous. And she was never warm enough; he had discovered that immediately. But now — it would be good for her to review the situation objectively; she had to protect herself; she was profoundly vulnerable, abnormally sensitive, easily frightened. The facts: she had awakened crying; she had shyly touched him; he had refused her. He, who had once craved her so relentlessly. Then she would just have to distance herself, to protect herself from more damage while playing the role of satisfied wife and planning her escape. Many men would give anything to receive the least caress from her; she could honestly say that at least a dozen in the fellowship were in love with her. All right, she'd play the role because she was not a fickle person, she'd meet her obligations, but please don't ask her to wear the sweater, to endure the pain of that, to be reminded of his indifference when she offered her love wholeheartedly. Yes, that's how she chose to face the situation; she could choose another view, she could force herself into the rigid way of a saint (how often she had to warn the fellowship about that!) and put on the sweater to please him. But then that would be false, and she wanted to spend every precious second of her mortal life in truth.

She made her way through blouses, sweaters, and dresses, the hangers scraping an atonal song on the metal bar. I cannot betray myself, even if God Himself were to ask me. . . . Almost no one saw the sculptures on the roofs of cathedrals, but the artisans had toiled to make them flawless. For God . . . (something that showed off her legs in case Kuno appeared but that nevertheless seemed ministerial when Suzanne, the music director, came to call). Never would she follow the lifeless, hypocritical path of her father. When she took up his profession, she did so with the vow that she would constantly place herself in conditions that demanded truth, and (here was the black silk blouse with mother-of-pearl buttons) she had succeeded to a great degree; one had only to look to all the others who were genuinely affected by her example.

She put on the blouse, which she had bought for herself the day after Kuno had told her goodbye forever. It had been her task to say it: "So this is goodbye forever." He remained silent, jingling coins in the pocket of his windbreaker. As she closed the car door, he muttered something about hoping to stay friends. Friends!

Again she observed herself rummaging. Hurry, search!

From underneath a stack of underwear she drew a velvet-upholstered box and opened it with a soft snap. In its rosy satin interior lay an antique red-gold band, which she slipped on her little finger, as Kuno had diligently placed it on her finger the night that — yes, she was correct to think of it this way — the night that her life had changed. Irrevocably. *Bom, bom-pa-dum, bom!* Only a gold trinket, when he could afford diamonds. Off it had come forever after she had seen Kuno kissing an extremely attractive, deep-breasted, much younger woman in front of the Italian café in the city, where he always met Melpomene. A gray-eyed socialite, according to Ruth, named Janine. Melpomene was not a jealous person, of course, but she wanted the woman to die.

Melpomene stood before the canted mirror above the chest of drawers, sucked in her stomach, and turned in profile to her best side. During her lunch break she would buy the dress as a surprise; never at her weddings would she have been so bourgeois as to wear white, and it was her custom to appear in dark hues. (She hadn't wished Janine ill because of hatred — no, she thought, I am not conventional; it was simply that the stupid woman had been bad for Kuno, for his art.) And she would rearrange her hair — henna it, draw it in points over her forehead the way she had as a girl. And she would tightly close the door on the dream, on the startling blur behind her.

Weight shifted from foot to foot, floorboards creaked, breath, breath, pictures formed inside two heads in the house, formed and dissolved, formed and dissolved.

What did Schubert mean by that music? James scrubbed the stove clean of the scum of burned milk. He placed two mugs on the counter and poured the coffee. What did Schubert intend, when the music lifts up from the instrument and seems about to form itself into words, as if someone stood on a mountain, on a precipice before a storm, calling out over the sea, calling, and below, the waves were roiling up, green and white, and the horizon was blackening? It would be necessary really to listen to the Impromptu, uncritically, openly. He means something, he means something, but he doesn't allow it to become language. Calling, calling.

Bom, bom-pa-dum, bom. . . . . James ought to investigate this. A rumbling of bass arpeggios. The aroma of coffee, the keyboard, the precipice, the turbulent ocean, the feet, the heads, the house: none of this would last. But perhaps the phrase would endure, the phrase into which the composer had poured all his being, and on some other planet in a million years, someone would ask, What does he mean by that? This gave James an inexplicable pleasure. The paintings of Mauritius gave him this, too. And what were the paintings saying? He understood, but he didn't know how or with what he was able to comprehend; some other self grasped what Mauritius intended by a woman gazing over her shoulder. How to bring that self through the occluded glass wall behind which it hid, how to bring the two selves into rapport, into words? He would ask Melpomene for suggestions.

From below: "Darling, the coffee is made. Would you like some toast?"

From above: "I don't think so, dear."

The bay wrinkled and smoothed itself under a warm, cloudless sky. He could have invented games to play the rest of the day. Indians, Pirates, Space Aliens. If a big hand had picked him up and set him down at his desk and pointed to the stack of photocopied documents and the trays of slides, he would have flailed about and screamed and tried to escape. As it was, the sun swept him, mug in hand, into the garden, which smelled of crushed herbs and fermenting apples, and on down the slope, past the hedgerow and field, to the bay. He skipped a flat stone across the water — two hits and it sank. Five hits was the best he'd ever done, in the days when he thought nothing of spending an afternoon at it, but his best friend had often achieved seven hits.

No matter. Today James would work. Of course he was also entitled to walk around on his own property. No one would stop him from that. This was America, and the air in his lungs was pure, and he was a good person. Melpomene had said so. Of course she indulged him, and her assurances sometimes made him feel a little foolish, but she knew him inside and out, and maybe she was right. A pair of swans rose and fell on the blue swells, silver and white, silver and white. Farther out bobbed a flock of migrating shore birds — merganser, or brant, or black duck; he should have brought his field glasses. The light, a tinge bluer than a week ago, was so strong that the clear atmosphere became a magnifying lens, and he could distinguish leaves, yellow and red and gold, on the branches of oaks on a distant point. Too cold for swimming; that was finished.

Annoying pedants might have made bigger names for themselves than he had, but they did not own this land. The house was his, the garden his, the marsh grass his, the birds, the sailboat rounding the point, and perhaps even the long-legged tanned woman at the tiller was his, and the shredded piece of translucent moon as well. A woman, standing in her bath, had glanced over her shoulder, the radiance of what she had just seen lingering in her eyes.

He spun on one foot, and everything became new: the weathered shingles of the house, the mottled foliage under the cedars, the dark green depths where the lawn met the woods, the tree trunks slashed with shadow, the yellow field. The day pivoted around him, welcoming, new and whole and fragrant. But he could not call his friends to come over to help build a fort or bury pirate treasure; today they would not walk shirtless on the sides of their feet, as braves along deer trails among the pines. Those crisp mornings when he and his friends rapidly settled on what the game would be and their roles! The shorter the summer got, the more intense and convoluted their play became; he refused to return to the house when called, and they stayed on, shivering into the twilight until they were compelled to come indoors. He and the others understood, without saying it, that when one of them left, the world lost its depth and exhilaration and became a mere game, which they listlessly played, just as they understood that as soon as someone refused his role ("I don't want to be the Indian anymore, I want to be Captain Kidd") the walls of the game grew thin and they could see through them to an ordinary house inhabited by ordinary parents on the usual grassy slope going down to the everyday bay with its modern sailboats and motor launches. And each of them abruptly became ordinary boys, bored, making absurd gestures. (In recollection it seemed to him that he and the others had actually worn buckskin trousers and carried long rifles or bows.) Their bodies had enlarged and taken them to law firms and banks and wives and golf and other sober accomplishments. And he himself ought to achieve something lasting, to behave like a man. When he had married Melpomene, a real woman, he felt himself taller and more serious. At last, in middle age, he had taken up what his father had called a man's estate. But why wasn't it as interesting, as real, as those old games? Because it was prescribed, because everyone expected something important of James? Because Melpomene had encouraged him so strongly to study Mauritius? But that was to help him grow; she must have seen some subtle connection between him and the artist. Maybe for Mauritius painting was only an absorbing form of child's play, and if James could transform the project into a game. . . .

The porch lamp blinked off. She kept it on all night because she believed that it discouraged burglars from coming down the long lane to their house and killing them. When she began to stay with him, he would hear her walking around downstairs in the night, turning the bolts; she asked him to put chains on the doors and locks on the windows. Surprised, he laughed. She was fearless about hurtling herself into soup kitchens and shelters in the most vicious slums, and she was willing to receive any visitor, no matter how suspect. But one night she told him detailed stories of murder and theft until he was terrified and promised her locks and a burglar alarm. He couldn't sleep and wanted her company, but she lay down peacefully beside him and dozed off.

He headed toward the porch, happy at the thought that he might find her there, her hand still on the switch perhaps, looking out at the bay. He would hold her; thank her for that delightful question this morning: What do you want today? He would try hard to guess exactly what she desired; she could usually guess that for him. He wanted to make her the perfect meal, to tempt her to eat, to give her the pleasure of that; she worked so hard for others. Then afterward, if she was free, they would go for a stroll. When she had moved in, she had said, "Every day we'll walk for an hour, hand in hand." But the new fellowship had kept her busy, and it took her longer and longer to deal with visitors, compose her sermons — her talks, and to answer her mail (sometimes she would come out of her study saying she had spent the entire day writing one letter to someone who had asked her counsel; people even corresponded from abroad). And he would remind her, too, of their plan to drive north for a few days and stay at an inn, and hike in the autumn forests. She badly needed the rest.

As he entered the vestibule, which was clammy and smelled of old cordwood and rubber boots, he contracted. His punishment was to spend the day indoors. He had been summoned, year after year, breathless from play, hands and cheeks chafed, to come in and eat, or study, or go to bed. Adults had to stay indoors and work. They had to do their chores and be responsible. (The switch was on; she hadn't been here after all.) They had to change burned-out bulbs and fix lunch; they had to convince others to be responsible. Otherwise, James said sternly to himself, the universe would fail.

When he stepped into the kitchen, he found Melpomene hugging herself and whirling so that her flowered skirt fanned out. She did not see him. Smiling, he retreated.

*

"Oh, Kuno," she whispered to herself. His plane would pass over this very house. And it would not crash. (If he died, she would not want to live, and she was in terror of dying.) No. It would descend gently to the earth, because — she smiled at her superstition — it carried him. And he would phone her. Would she take the call? Probably. She would be soft. Or no, a little remote, requiring apologies and pledges, asserting her unshakable love for James — how constant he was, how considerate! — before she would release her warmth and forgiveness. From now on, she would no longer be the slave; after all, he needed her. His letter was the proof. But suppose it crashed — there, in the field. Then she would race to the wreckage. James would call to her that it might explode, but she wouldn't stop, she would be thinking only of saving Kuno's life, of stanching the blood with a strip torn from her skirt, of dragging him to safety. To the television cameras she would say, ignoring her own injuries, "I could not do otherwise!" And of course no one would know that the wounded stranger was her lover.

Through the window she saw James teetering on a deck chair, reaching for the bulb in the porch lamp. "What are you doing?" she shouted. "That's no way! You'll hurt yourself." She ran downstairs to the basement (hurry, hurry), cobwebs brushing her face, found the ladder, and carried it up to the porch, her spine swaying. As she set the ladder down, it banged her leg. "See what you made me do?" She lifted her skirt. Tears filled her eyes. "Now I have a bruise, an ugly bruise." Horrible. Kuno would see it.

James came down from the chair in a long, alarmed step, bulb in hand, and examined the red mark. "Poor baby. I am so sorry! I didn't mean —" It was not, in the sunlight, the thigh he was accustomed to thinking of as hers: the muscle loose, a web of tiny purple veins under a film of pale skin. "I don't believe it's a bruise, though. It doesn't look too —"

The phone in her study rang, and she rushed indoors.

Why had he been so stupid? Why had he caused her pain? Until he met her, he hadn't realized how savage he could be; or rather, how savage his unconscious was. She had been compelled to indicate to him, out of kindness, all the ways he secretly wished to harm her, in his dreams, in his careless acts. It distressed her to have to speak about these matters, she said, but she wanted to help him become more aware. He left his books stacked by the chair in the sun-room, where she could trip over them; he used her slide projector, and afterward she couldn't work it properly; when he had borrowed her car, someone had backed into the fender (he still refused to accept her interpretation of this; he had felt no anger toward her at all that day; the accident, he silently held, was not his fault; maybe the dent was even already there; but often she sensed his intentions before he did, so perhaps she was right); she had to return almost every gift he had ever given her, so obtuse was he in his choices. Dropping into the deck chair, he slapped the gray bulb, its filaments rattling, against his palm. Alice. He could call her. He would whisper: Please.

At his back he heard the crunch of tires on gravel. He quickly stepped inside before the visitor could see him.

Three

"SO EARLY in the morning." Melpomene, coffee mug in hand, let Kristen in from the waiting room. She hated people dropping by unexpectedly; now all the taut threads of the planned day threatened to go slack and snarl. Kristen and everyone else in the fellowship knew they were to set up appointments in advance. But Melpomene made her face smooth. "Why didn't you phone?"

Kristen was wearing a wrinkled dress, and she had a red welt along her cheek, as if she had slept on a rock. "I'm very sorry, Reverend," she said, her voice tremulous. "I didn't mean to disturb — I'll go. I just wanted to tell you one —"

"Oh, come along, dear." Melpomene beamed and put a hand on Kristen's shoulder and conducted her into the study. Kristen was one of the gentlest members of the fellowship. "Quickly, now — I've got other people scheduled."

"I . . . I won't take too much of your —" Kristen sat on the edge of the sofa. A leaf lay on the carpet. She blinked.

The blink lasted a night and a day. The birds wove an intricate song with holes of silence, holes in the sky itself. She clung to the leather-upholstered arm. The Reverend, enthroned next to the angel on the pedestal, was powerful, beautiful, erect. She tilted her head slightly, indicating that she had already perceived Kristen's message: time is a substance. If Kristen said it outright the world would hear and punish her. But the proof was uttered by the sofa — recently the trunk of a tree, the hide of a living animal, the iron in a rock, now the object whispering to her cells. Instead she said, "I saw him. I couldn't sleep. Gabriel."

Kristen was ravishing as well as intelligent; Melpomene would take care that Kuno never saw her. Although she appeared pale and exhausted, her skin exuded a faint radiance, her eyes were large and limpid, her hair curly and fair. "Have you been driving around again, Kristen?"

You, Kristen, driving. The words, perfectly formed waves breaking and foaming, were directed toward the body here on the sofa who had once been a tenth of a millimeter long and was at present five and a half feet. Kristen: yes, that was what she was called, but who she was, was — think; it was important not to seem crazy — the woman who loved Gabriel. Gabriel, gone for years, now living not three miles from here. And who was that woman who loved him? The woman everyone called Kristen, and that was what the Reverend had called her, and so she must behave like Kristen. Better to keep quiet about this. The world did not want you to know how it worked; that was why it always deflected language. But the secret had to be passed on. She must not forget: time is composed of infinitely small particles driven at us by a high wind; its velocity is so great that we can never perceive it; we're always leaning into the storm; the particles become embedded in us. Is there no escape? Refuse, resist! That was what she must convey to the Reverend.

"I thought we were finished with that business."

Finished . . . yes, Kristen was finished. The Reverend had spoken the truth. The sky was finished, the trees. The leaf was dying around the edges; the heart still burned green.

"You saw Gabriel, then? He's living here now, in the Wyatt mansion?" Melpomene had heard about the absent, touring celebrity ever since her arrival. "And afterward you couldn't sleep? And you started driving?"

"Just for a few . . . days. I ran out of gas." Kristen had received a very good sign: she went into an unlocked house, and she knew it was where she belonged, it was the house for her, and the bed was just for her, and she slept and had only good dreams, caused by the fog coming in the window. She was awakened by children around her bed — they were Gabriel's and hers, it was the future, and everything was going to turn out all right; time could be refused. "Reverend, I found a bed that was safe, and there's no reason to be afraid. Nothing is going to happen to us that hasn't already happened to someone." The woman had told her to leave, and that was a sign, too, that she needed to be free of houses. Free of houses, then free of others, then of herself: that was the procedure, and it was important to go step by step. "I went to Gabriel again because he's not well. He needs you. I'm the bridge. We talked. He used to stay up all night telling me his theories. He said he doesn't have theories anymore. I told him he ought to go sleep in that house. Really, it would make him unbelievably happy. I told him to come and see you." Kristen sank back; she had been on the sofa, oh, years now, and had been distracted from its message by her busy chatter. She inhaled, and the leaf moved along the carpet.

Melpomene nodded. "Let me see if I follow. Your mind is rushing along, you've been driving around like you used to do when you couldn't sleep, and sleeping in strange places, and you're worried about Gabriel."

"Yes." Remarkable how the pictures in Kristen's mind flowed through the air and reassembled themselves in the Reverend's mind, which was the same as the mind of God, which lay in the leaf there, the leaf pitted by the merciless wind.

"And you need to eat, and to rest, and to stop thinking for a while. Isn't that so?"

A silence. "Yes."

"And you want to stop feeling so — so confused."

"Yes."

"And you came here to tell me Gabriel might pay me a visit, and you came here because you know I can help you."

"Yes."

"Because I've helped you before, and it worked very well, and you were quiet and calm then. Remember? To live one second at a time, just like we're doing now, going from one second to the next, on a straight, easy path. . . ."

But the path, the path filled the room, and was oppressed on all sides by the walls of dead trees, and the wind blew.

"Kristen?"

"Please, please help Gabriel. He's lost."

"All right, I can try. What can we do that will be useful? I'm sure you have the answer, if you just let it rise to the surface."

It was cool in the study, and Melpomene's blouse was thin, but she didn't dare interrupt to get a sweater. Kristen might interpret that as a lack of solicitude. Perhaps Melpomene would wear her sable, if she consented to meeting Kuno. The sable from James that she had chosen thinking of Kuno (perhaps he'd turn up at lectures James would give one day at the museum, say, or at some art institute, after he recaptured his eminence). Seeing her in that coat, he would recognize that she was more necessary to him than his other women.

Kristen stared at the carpet, her lips moving slightly. Poor darling. Melpomene had helped her find a job and assigned her the task of arranging flowers for the meetinghouse, and lately she had even started attending the philosophy-group luncheons. And now this old lover, a musician of some sort, was ruining all Melpomene's efforts.

At the end, when Kuno said he had decided to be frank, he announced that he wanted to pour all his energy into his career; he was tired of being overlooked. Melpomene had known — because she knew everything; it was terrible to have this gift — that he meant he wanted a younger, prettier woman. (*That* woman, with her tasteless displays of public lust.) With money and position. An ugly thing, this trait. But a painter needed to think like that, to make social connections, and Kuno had developed the habit before he'd met Melpomene. It was the residue of a time when he had been hungry, when he had not yet experienced real love, not yet written her the letters declaring that all he lived for was to create a work of art worthy of her. And so why not marry for practical reasons in the meantime? But at the moment she didn't care about his history. She wanted only to appear splendid when they met again (past and future ceased; how

39

he and she had blended into one another!). Yes, she would let him beg her, and then she would agree to see him. And it was James's fault, really; the blame lay with him if she again opened herself helplessly to Kuno, wearing the gold ring, the new dress, the sable, the lapis lazuli necklace James had given her.

But just look at how she had wandered, she had almost forgotten Kristen, forlornly clutching the arm of the sofa. Oh, and she had been making such progress lately! She required protection; she might even need treatment (a problem: psychiatrists had tormented the girl; only through Melpomene had she found real succor). It would be good to observe her closely for a while. "Have you come up with any answers?"

"Gabriel has changed. He used to be so handsome. But time —" She stopped. The leaf veins were dying, the heart glow was fading, because she was breathing, because she was about to let the secret slide out. "I think if I took care of him he might be healthier."

"My dear, you know how fond I am of you. It may be that you can do something for Gabriel, and it's very considerate of you to want that, especially after the way I think he's treated you. But what about you? You can't go on these driving binges. You can't walk into people's houses and sleep in their beds. What you're searching for, you won't find in that way."

"Do you think I'll ever be with Gabriel?" (And out of time's wind?)

"First you have to be with yourself. I see you've been absorbed in studying the carpet. Did you know it's called a tree-of-life rug? A very ancient motif. Look at the pairs of

40

birds there, in the branches. One looks on while the other eats the fruit. You could think that each pair forms a whole person. You know that already, but you've temporarily forgotten. Together, let's remember. How can we help Kristen, all the parts of Kristen?"

Melpomene used to put on her mother's pearls and her fur when her parents were away, and sit cross-legged in the center of this very carpet, in the crown of the tree of life, with its bright birds and colored leaves, her eyes squeezed shut, praying aloud, amazing the impressionable nanny. Melpomene's father — he had given her that cumbersome name when he was studying Greek in divinity school — did not believe in prayer. It was infantile, he always said, to ask God for anything. How could someone who had so clearly lacked a calling, to whom a cathedral had never spoken, dare assert anything about God? Suppose a prayer were a deep wish, and you kept repeating it until your whole being was magnetized. She had longed to meet a man like Kuno, and one day there he was, next to her on the plane. . . . But her father — so pompous! And her mother — why, why? But she would not be vexed today; anyway, she had long ago given up analyzing them. To analyze, to explain, is to lie. Instead, she had simply said yes to everything, and there, by the way, was a good topic for a talk.

Kristen looked out the window. A flock of little birds fluttered down to a branch. Seeing the shivering of leaves, the incandescent tunnels among the boughs, the shadow of her hand lifting to brush her eyes, they sprang up again.

The Reverend at last spoke. "What are you feeling?"

Love and joy brimmed from each of her words. And each held a thousand echoing glassy shapes, one inside the next, and each one was strung on a shining fiber that reached all the way back to the first words ever to leave a human mouth, and all the way forward to the final ones gasped out by the last human. The wondrous, flashing net undulated in the air. So beautiful, so unbidden, and Kristen so undeserving! She wept.

"No crying, now. That's not good for you. We can't waste tears. We have to save them for the big things, remember? Now let's go over what we've talked about all these months — how you need to rest, and eat, and keep calm." The Reverend's voice, as soft as sand blowing along the shore. "You were doing very well until you found out about Gabriel. You'd come to an acceptance about him. Think. You can do that again. You have a lovely house, your garden that you've made so beautiful, you have your teaching job that gives you so much satisfaction, the school plays that everyone adores so much, you have your friends in the fellowship. And you have me. What's missing? It's you, yourself, the inner you — waiting for you, calling to you. We mustn't let ourselves be moved by external forces. In a way, our own moods, our own thoughts, are external forces. Our own brains."

"External forces killed Christ."

"Christ knew His destiny. He faced it without flinching."

On the other side of the glass, once sand, now a transparent rigid pane, the leaves of trees, which had been hyphens of information on a pair of twining strands within a seed, twittered. A rabbit, which had recently been nothing but a speck, bounded across the field, which had just been under the ocean. The relentless wind. But she must act normal, she must be Kristen. "Gabriel used to hold me, and then I could

42

sleep. But things have changed so completely, everything is slipping past, it's too much . . ."

How still Melpomene felt, how aware, how balanced, how abundant! Other lives were ghastly. Terrible that people lived in a waking nightmare! That was why she would never leave the ministry, never give up her vocation, never break the vow she had made in the cathedral.

The Reverend got up and sat beside Kristen and put her arm around her shoulders. "I'm here, I'm with you, don't worry. You've felt like this before and you've courageously pulled yourself together. See if you can find the solid ground, the peace."

Kristen closed her eyes. To be so close to the Reverend! In the dark Kristen tried to will her inner self to appear; but all she could find were hurtling galaxies, nebulae, the spewing furnace from which all matter streamed.

"I sense your tiredness, Kristen. Why don't you go home, to your own bed, and sleep? And maybe later you'll want to work in your garden, and that's a fine place to discover what's good in change, in growth. And you can be wondering what's helpful — to you, to Gabriel — and we'll discuss that."

"I didn't want to bother you. I didn't remember if this was your day to see people. I was wrong not to make an appointment."

"Kristen, dear, you never bother me. We all have days like this sometimes. You have a problem of a certain size. It's not an overwhelming one, even though it might seem that way at moments. We can solve it. The fact that you came to me means you're ready to end it. You know that I'm battling for your happiness with everything I've got. I'll never stop. I understand what you're going through. It's fine that Gabriel may make an appointment — you did tell him to call first? But we can't expect any magic. At the moment you're stuck, but you can really explore how stuck you are, be conscious of that, and then you can be free. Do you want to hear a story?"

Kristen loved the Reverend's stories. She nodded and let her head rest against the Reverend's shoulder. Day, then night, then day, then night.

"Once there was an Indian tribe. And the people believed if someone drew a circle in the dirt around a person, then he could not possibly get out." The Reverend's voice became low, rhythmical, and soothing, and Kristen could feel the vibrations in her throat and collarbone. "The person would stand there, helpless, unable to step over the line in the dirt. Can you imagine? He believed that circle would hold him forever. Someone would have to come and erase part of it so he would be released. Do you understand? It was nothing but a circle drawn in the dirt, but for him it was a prison. What do you think?"

Kristen sat up. She was here, calm, level, back on the surface. Sheltered. Behind the Reverend's large, liquid eyes stretched an ocean of wisdom. She wore the rippling blouse of the night sea.

"Any questions, Kristen?" The Reverend bent over and picked up the corroded leaf and twirled it.

What had she come to tell the Reverend? She couldn't recall. The Reverend led her outside and tossed the leaf on the ground. Kristen snatched it up.

"It is pretty, isn't it? Still half green." The Reverend opened the car door for Kristen. "Seems to be getting a bit

brisk. One day it's summer, the next day fall. Don't you
have a jacket?"

Kristen shrugged.

"Wait — I'll be right back." The Reverend disappeared.

Kristen pressed the leaf against her chest. Sun filtered
down through the trees. The day was friendly and sweet,
hiding its storm under a smooth skin of blue and gold.

"I think you're my size, dear. Here." A violet angora
sweater spilled out of the Reverend's arms into Kristen's lap.

"Oh, Reverend!" For no reason at all, this tremendous
bounty; ah, Kristen was blessed. The Reverend seemed
taller than a minute ago.

"Wonderful, wonderful. That color suits you. Now go
home and sleep."

James picked up a stack of notes. He would study hard; he
would learn all there was to know. He could: the proof was
in the documents (his miraculous discovery, in the archives
of the Guild of St. Luke in Delft, of the record of the estate
of Reynier Vermeer, father of the painter, listing three
panels, *Adam and Eve, The Crucifixion, The Kingdom of
Heaven* — all now lost — by Mauritius), the books, the trays
of slides, the humming computer, the patina of the rosewood desk, the sun pricking out deep blue and rust and
ocher geometry in the carpet, Mauritius's *Girl Bathing* looking over her shoulder at him, her mouth slightly open, the
folds of the white, lace-trimmed garment she held to her
breast tinged gold by a beam that fell from a high window.
No one could paint lace like Mauritius; his technique was
almost arrogant. Would it be too daring to imply that Rembrandt had learned the trick from Mauritius, who traveled

back and forth between Delft and Amsterdam and who, James was about to declare, was the tutor of Vermeer and Fabritius as well? But even if James successfully proved his case, even if he vanquished the critics who were waiting in ambush, still he might never know why Mauritius (just a name; who was the man?) chose to dedicate himself to making these few elusive works of art, and he might die without ever understanding them. And yet the certainty of understanding pulled at him, at the self on the other side of the clouded pane, the self to whom the paintings were speaking.

Over the field, Melpomene's hawk circled. Crows cawed and cut across its path, wings almost brushing wings. Why did the crows resent the presence of the hawk? Weren't they scavengers? Wouldn't the hawk be searching out live prey? Did the hawk ever catch anything? James had observed only restless circling. But of course, to survive it must kill. That was rooted in its essence, and nothing could legislate otherwise, least of all James's hope that nature was benign.

Under his feet, speech vibrated. Low, steady, feminine voices. Some days a sob or a shout or a laugh would rise up from Melpomene's study; alien emotions, like unwholesome fumes, would leak through the floorboards and the Heriz carpet, which she had found at an estate sale and put down to muffle his tread.

What had happened to the immediacy, the clarity that the dream had given him? The gates had flown open for an instant. He had known something. He pushed the books away and clapped on his headphones. The Schubert Impromptu: a mountaineer, full of enterprise, setting out on a morning climb. James must take the time to listen to the piece, absorb it. But his eye fell on the diary: close-grained leather, marbleized endpapers. A gift from her, along with the rosewood paper box and the antique silver cup with its thicket of pens and pencils. And the Mauritius reproduction — what a coup. Seldom could you find reproductions of his work. What a wizard she was!

Now, where was he? He had been swimming through Canaletto waters, warm and bright and ridged; the girl had turned and contemplated him; he had known then how to begin. He awakened lucid and in order. (If anyone else had reported such a visit to a realm of pure beauty, James would have secretly — or perhaps in print — ridiculed him.) A true painting was a machine that enabled you to enter eternity. Yes, that was how it felt. But the aura of the dream was fading. In the fifteenth century the average European saw in his entire lifetime only three man-made images. What astonishment a painting must have evoked in the medieval brain! He sat down at the desk and put his thumb to his teeth. He picked up a pen. The mountaineer was in despair. Would he ever reach the summit? A rippling sensation in James's gut made him put the pen down. This happened nearly every day, and then he would prowl in search of a book, or go for a walk, or look for Melpomene, and she could always sense that he was in anguish again, and she would repeat to him some practical bit of information — remind him, for instance, to break the task down into small segments and deal with each one separately. He took off the headphones. Maybe he lacked the intelligence for this enterprise; he was not an academically trained art scholar. He had deceived Melpomene about his talents, or she assumed too much.

A door closed below. He craved the days when she would stay home from her ministerial conferences, her hospital rounds, but then strangers appeared and disappeared in the drive and on the lawn at all hours, visiting his wife in her stronghold. Her rule was they must never see him. They had to feel free to weep or shout or confess with only Melpomene as the witness. She enlisted him as her tacit collaborator in creating this haven; she told him how, when her father was dying and the slightest noise sent him into nervous anguish, she and her mother learned to move and communicate soundlessly, and how this practice had led her to perfect an inner silence of great richness. Naturally, he wanted that as well; he envied the variety of experiences and disciplines she had managed to acquire.

What did she hear on visitors' day? What did she say? Even though she had not been here all that long, the members of the fellowship were already devoted to her. They stopped by with desserts and bouquets; the grounds committee offered to mow the lawn and prune the shrubbery; a woman named Ellen tucked one-hundred-dollar bills into little volumes of poetry and left them in the mailbox.

He lay down on the carpet to do some posture exercises Melpomene had shown him not long after they became lovers. He was tall, but he stooped, which she felt gave him an insecure air.

Her phone had begun ringing; if she forgot to turn the sound off it would ring almost continuously the whole day. "Oh, my God!" Her voice — elated. "What? This is a bad connection. You can't try again? . . . You're *in the air?* . . . I'll try to talk louder. But I have to be extremely careful. . . . I said, I have to be careful."

James rolled on his side, held his breath, and pressed his ear to the rug.

A long pause. "What?" And louder: "Of course, dearest
. . . still love . . . meet *immediately* . . . bye."

He lay curled up, staring at the baseboard, until the wool
of the rug made his cheek itch, and then he got to his feet,
stood with his arms at his sides, slapped his flanks twice and
expelled air in a rapid stream through his lips. A cloud of
geese lifted from the bay, honking, flying low, departing.

His hand roamed through the stacks of lace underwear.
What were these things, and whenever did she wear them?
Here was a ring box; he'd seen that before. In the mirror,
beyond his head and shoulders, stretched the plain of the
bed.

If he could find a name, proof, evidence. He did not know
which man it was whom she still loved and planned to meet,
and so it could be any man — any man who came to the
house, any man in the fellowship, in the village, or on the
train, or in the streets of the city, in the restaurants, in
the museums. In the air, for God's sake. There were men
everywhere, most of them far more successful and powerful
than he, and she had chosen one of their number. Any given
man was more to her than he was. All the other men in the
world had annihilated him. She had said to him after their
wedding: I am finished with all my imbecilities about men.
He was the victor that day; he had won her. I am home at
last, she said. Here I stay. That night he had carried her up
the stairs to this bed: now the house would have a life; now
the crops would grow.

His fingertips struck something hard under the perfumed
satin. A shell. A scallop shell. A faint iridescence lined its
interior. Why would she keep a scallop shell in her drawer?

He ran his thumb over the nacreous curves. Why the flicker of a rainbow on the inside of something that remained hidden in muddy shallows until after the lump of flesh it housed was dead? Anyway, she valued it enough to store it among her intimate things. He shoved the treasure in his pocket and quickly shut the drawer. What if she were to catch him? What would he say? That he was in agony, desperate to know the truth?

Melpomene entered the kitchen, rubbing the bridge of her nose. "Oh, there you are." To make him think she had been searching anxiously for him.

He touched the shell in his pocket. Maybe he would casually say, This anything of yours? I found it on the bedroom floor. Or perhaps, Is someone we know airborne at the moment? But she was pale, and two creases furrowed her forehead. A tremendous strain weighed on her. "Are you all right?" he asked, disconcerted. "Would you like something to eat?"

She stared off into the middle distance and shook her head. "Mother — Mother could be dead."

"What?" His heart knotted. He went to her. "What happened?"

"She's threatening suicide again. I don't know!"

"Oh, God, darling — you mean she's still just — she's all right at the moment? You had me very scared there. Do you think she's serious?"

"She loves the idea of dying. She said the other day that it would be the only way for her to find out the truth. What a hysteric. I don't know. She wants me to come."

"We — we should go then."

"Oh, no, no. I wouldn't dream of interrupting you — you wanted to work today."

"I haven't started yet. We can go immediately."

She avoided his eyes, put her chin down, and spoke slowly. "I have no time whatsoever. I'm completely booked. I still have to write my talk, I've got people coming the entire day." Her voice rose to a higher register. "But I suppose I should visit her. Maybe tonight. Spend the night with her. The poor old thing, sitting there — yes, sitting there on her brocade sofa and brooding over Father's sermons. Can't you just see her, full of venom and feeling sorry for herself? She doesn't have anyone around to frighten anymore so she frightens herself. She's got the stamina, she's got the will — she could do it."

"Let's go. I can drive you. That way you'd get a few hours' rest. You could work on your talk in the car —" The serrated edge of the shell could probably cut flesh; didn't the Indians use shells as knives?

"No, no — you're too busy. Don't bother about me. I'll manage. Really. I'll just — oh, there's my next lost sheep in the driveway."

"You look very pretty today, Reverend," Suzanne said. "Something good must be happening."

Melpomene smiled and clasped Suzanne's hands. "Sit down, please." Suzanne started to sit in the leather chair. "No," said Melpomene. "There, on the sofa." The Reverend took the leather chair.

Suzanne, who played harpsichord and piano at the church and who favored teardrop pearl earrings and raw silk suits, had never sought Melpomene's guidance, and this was the first compliment she had ever paid her. Everyone else in the fellowship had quickly come to appreciate Melpomene's capabilities and was not shy about speaking of them to her and to others. Suzanne — what had held her back? Hidden aggression, of course. She never consulted Melpomene about what pieces would be best, and in fact firmly ignored her suggestions. Would Suzanne play the Prelude and Fugue No. 12 from Book 2 of *The Well-Tempered Clavier?* Never, even though Melpomene gave her the score. No, Suzanne appeared with her own sheaf of music, she played Scarlatti and Albinoni with precision, perhaps a bit weightily, and after the services she went out on the lawn behind the meetinghouse for a cigarette, and, as she said goodbye, she always had a gallingly brilliant smile for James.

"What can I do for you today?"

"Well, I just felt — I need — I need to talk to you, Reverend," Suzanne said, bowing her head.

Suzanne's submissive gesture stirred tendrils of helpful energy in Melpomene's heart. She made her expression receptive and concerned. "What is it, dear?"

"It's my health. I've been unwell, out of breath for several months. Usually there was a good reason — the flu, getting overtired."

"Oh, that's really too bad. What could it be? Are you under some sort of stress?" Suzanne was heavy about the hips, and there was a bit of a hump forming between her shoulders already — no man would care for that in bed — and then there was her smug manner. But of course James, probably thrilled with her smile, would be blind to such details. "Have you seen a doctor?"

"I made excuses to myself for months, but finally I had a

checkup. The doctor ran some tests and X rays, and he told me there was a spot on my lung —"

"A spot on your lung. Yes." There it was. Best just to say it out, to face it. Suzanne had made herself ill because she was constricted. Suzanne would die, then, and Melpomene would be called upon to conduct the service. To select the Bach to be played. Death. Right here in her study. Oh, why couldn't Suzanne be someone else, here to ask about a wedding, a christening? Only yesterday Melpomene had cupped her hand over the downy scalp of the Garretts' new baby and sprinkled a few drops of water on his head and wished with all her might that the child grow in peace, and she told the parents that she had the intuition that she would know that baby all her life. But Suzanne was staring at her with hard eyes like marbles. "I'm terribly sorry —"

"He told me not to jump to conclusions. At the moment all we know is that there's a shadow in the upper left lobe. I didn't think about the spot much at first. I didn't mention it to anyone. Then last night I was walking down Main Street, and I realized that I was probably going to have a knife cutting into my chest, and that afterward I would feel pain. I would be the one feeling it. It didn't belong to any other person in the world, that pain waiting for me. I didn't want to tell anyone. I didn't know how. I didn't know how I could tell the news in such a way that I could prevent the people I cared about from becoming more frightened than I was. If they didn't know, then they weren't frightened at all."

"This has been a very hard time for you. You should have come to me immediately. I can help. You can fight this. We can fight this. I know people —"

"I thought if I kept it a secret, then it wouldn't really be happening to me."

Ah, you're just like me, Melpomene thought, and she loved Suzanne then, loved her enormously, and would certainly go with her to the hospital and be there in the recovery room when she awoke, and would hold her hand for as long as Suzanne required her.

Suzanne went on with her story. She had stopped in at a friend's house to tell her she was feeling a little lonely. The friend was giving a dinner for her ex-husband and some of their mutual friends. Suzanne, embarrassed, said hello and then left. "Her ex followed me out to the street and asked if something was wrong. He had a kind face. He put his hand on my shoulder. I told him everything was fine. But he knew. And it's the strangest thing. In that second I fell in love with him. All I think about is him. I don't know what to do."

"My dear, that's a sure sign that you're going to be well, you're going to be very, very well. We're going to make certain of that."

Four

THE SUN, reaching its off-center zenith, made the noon siren blast across the hedgerows, the fields, the marshes, the bay. Light weighed harshly on the bowed reeds, whose leaves ticked in the breeze. Branch shadows, firm and black, slithered through the garden. Penumbras of grass blades, spiky and transparent, shifted in minute increments. Raked here and there by cat's-paws, the bay glittered, and on its northern horizon, a solitary cloud rose up.

James stood at the edge of the lawn. His shadow, shrunken around his feet, was the size it had been at midday in the schoolyard. The air smelled of cedar and dried leaves. He was hungry. He had intended to eat a big breakfast, but Melpomene had gotten a bruise, and then he had gone upstairs and done — what? he couldn't remember — and then he had listened to her phone conversation, and even though her words probably meant nothing, he couldn't stop thinking about them, and now he had to ask himself whether Melpomene might lie to him, and for a while after she had upset him with the remark about her mother being dead, his appetite had vanished. But wasn't he lacking in facts? He needed to sit down with her at lunch. These brief intervals stolen between visitors were no good. Probably he was just imagining all kinds of ridiculous plots; he could plunge readily into nervous suspicion; before they were married he used to be racked by fantasies that she loved someone else, a prominent art critic, but she laughed with incredulity when he finally confessed, and soon afterward her eagerness for marriage washed the matter out of his head. Yes, now his mood lifted, and though it was true that he had overheard a cryptic exchange and that the air had taken on an edge, the day was still lovely and full of promise, and he was ravenous. In restaurants, Melpomene, understanding his urgency about food, would say merrily to the waiter, "Feed my husband immediately!"

Folding in upon himself, the curtain of indoor gloom falling around him, he entered the house. From Melpomene's study came the sounds of a woman weeping. Tear vapor seeped from under the door and pressed against his sinuses. Her day was one long sob. How did she endure it?

He tiptoed to the kitchen. He would wait for her. Sometimes she didn't care what he did about meals; other times, for no reason he had been able to learn, she became offended if he ate without her. True, most of the time he only thought about his own satisfaction; he lacked her driving wish to become a better person. She was justified in whispering the word "love" to someone, to "dearest," who was a superior, more thoughtful man than he. (Oh, but he had staked everything on her, relied on her direct, earthy manner, the strength in her hands when she squeezed his shoulder, the tears in her eyes when she said she would give her life for him.)

Alice had never promised him anything; as far as he could remember, she never told him how she felt about him, and he assumed she knew how much he cared for her. And she had never mentioned the abstract, the theoretical; she believed that works of art that were great were inhabited by a soul and embedded with hints indicating the way out of the ordinary world. If you opened your eyes, a dimension of beauty untouched by the daily disappointments inherent in being human would reveal itself. By her side he had stood until his knees ached, staring at Patinirs, Van Eycks, Holbeins, Rembrandts, Mauritiuses, Vermeers. Faces, a table, a rug, a bit of cloth, a goblet, a book, a knife glistened with sensibility. And as she pointed out these treasures, he would sometimes look instead at her; she had a profile like the Leonardo angel in *The Annunciation,* forceful, almost masculine, not altogether beautiful, but enormously clear and frank.

When he kissed her (so easily!) at a special exhibition of Giorgione's *The Tempest,* how was he to know that he was beginning something so vital and lasting? Why was it that just last night those feelings, long dormant, had suddenly awakened? His first marriage, to which he had sacrificed Alice (when he met her, the engagement had already been announced), had meanwhile come and gone, like some crowded, condensed, unrecoverable dream during an afternoon nap. With Melpomene, he had had to labor to get that first kiss, to endure many talks and conferences and dinner parties in the hope of spending a few minutes with her.

Sun glossed the twigs, many already bare, and flowed through the bay window and across the long pine table, illuminating the grain, making the salt and pepper shakers into monuments, touching the folds of the napkins and exposing their burden of crumbs and dark spots of grease. Melpomene neglected their laundering. He had once asked if they could have clean napkins daily. "There's nothing wrong with these — they're clean," she replied. "Do I have to do everything?" She had no time to wash napkins. She blamed the cleaning woman; she blamed his first wife for choosing such a bad cleaning woman, who could not be fired because she happened to be a member of the fellowship; she blamed him for having such poor judgment about women. The dirty napkins were his fault. He should have answered then and there, but he had been surprised and hurt. Now he thought: I don't ask much, and she's the one who insisted on cloth napkins. She could at least see to it that they were laundered. I am in my prime, strong, healthy, and this is what I have to think about? (*In the air! Dearest. Still love.*) She kept a seashell under her intimate things. And he had committed a theft, only a shell (the souvenir of an idyll?), but still. A thin blade of fear cut into his heart.

He fell past the minutes. The clock on the stove flashed 12:06. The hour is *this!* it said, the minutes are *that!* He rubbed his face. His cheeks had already lost their morning smoothness. (*Meet.*) His bones sank. But why start worrying now? Melpomene had always had her devotees, her divinity students, her philosophers and poets and artists. He sometimes said, "I have married an institution," and that pleased her. She was happiest when everyone begged her for wisdom, and she was especially challenged when he said to her that he did not know what to do with his life. Noting his enthusiasm for Mauritius, she suggested that the painter would be the ideal means for James's renaissance and said she would work with every fiber of her being on his behalf. She herself had never looked at the paintings, and James's instruction was the beginning of their love. He sat with her, inhaling her fragrance and turning the pages of an old collection of reproductions. When she listened, eyes fixed on him, the universe became dedicated solely to perpetuating his life; the rest of the world melted away; he and she rocked in a little boat in the center of the ocean.

The early fame James had gained through his trenchant articles and his book, an opinionated survey of twentieth-century Western culture, had evaporated, and now, she said, he ought to do something serious, something deep, something absolutely wonderful. On fire as never before, James agreed. He would achieve greatness so that one day she would sit in the front row at the lectures he would once again be invited to deliver, and smile up at him. Was there ever a more beautiful smile than the one she reserved for him when they were in public, the one that rendered him superior to everyone else present? And afterward she would stand beside him as people crowded around him. At the awards banquets, at the dinner parties, she would sit holding his hand, or perhaps touching his knee under the table.

But first he had to write the book, something worthy of her. He had learned enough Dutch to be able to read seventeenth-century documents; he made a pilgrimage to see every one of Mauritius's paintings. There were only twelve to be found, and one or two of those might be false attributions; after struggling with illness and debt, the poor devil had died at thirty-three when a powder magazine blew up and obliterated half of Delft. And how many other paintings had been lost or destroyed before his work at last began to be recognized, nearly three centuries later? Surely, James had a great mission, ratified by the discovery that he had made in the archives and that had been overlooked by all the specialists. It was up to him to establish the supreme importance of the master. That Vermeer, along with De Hooch, was a conscientious pupil of Mauritius's, himself a pupil of Rembrandt's, would be James's original contribution to human knowledge, sure to cause a stir; everyone had assumed for the last century that Bramer, a mediocre painter, was the sole tutor of the young Vermeer. But would James be brave enough? And how could he boldly make claims about Mauritius when he didn't even know the first thing about his own wife? She had given her attention, her smile, her soft words, to someone else. The world had dissolved, and James, the stolen shell in his pocket, with it.

Mauritius had lived, toiled, and died — that was all. If James had been born into a different family, in a different part of the world, he would probably have produced startling insights. If he had been reared, say, in a hut, he would have been able to speak eloquently about neglect, dirt, oppression, brittle palm leaves rattling, a muddy stream where women pounded clothes. He would have been able to contrast such a panorama with the calm breath of sky, water, brick, and gables that was Mauritius's *Canal Scene*. Or if James's father had been a lord, striding into the manor house in jodhpurs and snapping his fingers for brandy. . . . If James had chosen Alice instead.

Hunger overcame him. If only Melpomene would appear! He could ask her if she loved some other man. (Terror made his heart pound.) Resolve the thing. Only she could take his fear away; only she could guarantee that he had truly made her cry out with passion, that it had not all been an act. And if she refused? He would follow Alice's method, then; he would enter eternity, cleanse himself by spending his days meditating on the paintings of Mauritius until they surrendered their secrets. *Girl Bathing* (her poignant gaze, over her shoulder), *The Instruction of the Virgin* (that pure profile, the candlelight, the book), *Woman Weighing Gold* (the Madonna-like tranquillity, the string of pearls spilling out of the casket).

Melpomene came into the kitchen, her step light and brisk, and poured herself a mug of coffee.

James wanted to give her a pat, but he remained seated. "What about your mother? What are you going to do?" He would watch her face closely — a trick she had once shown him — to see if she was telling the truth.

She put down her cup and flung herself into his arms. Bewildered, he stroked her back.

She kissed him noisily on the cheek. "Oh, I have so much going on today! Kristen's old flame, that musician who has the Wyatt mansion, is coming, and there's my talk, and I've got to deal with some phone calls. Oh, your friend Suzanne dropped by — looks like lung cancer —"

"Suzanne?"

"Harpsichord."

"Oh, right. Lung cancer? What a shame."

Melpomene nodded. "If only she'd come to me sooner, I'm sure I could have helped her. But she's been so — I don't know — hunched, tight. She's aged, James, just in a week. But I'm going to do all I can. Oh, I am starving."

"Let's have some lunch right now."

"Oh, my dearest. My hungry boy." She rubbed his belly and he grinned. He squeezed her, and some papers in her skirt pocket crackled. "Lunch. Of course. Whatever you like. What would I do without you? So good! I just have to check my messages. I'll be back in a minute. You're right — I need to call Mother."

Melpomene loved anything old; she believed if only she had the time she could make a fortune restoring and reselling antiques picked up at flea markets. She told him tales of finding precious items like nineteenth-century cast-iron pig doorstops for next to nothing, or, in a gold-leaf frame, an illuminated Bible verse ("Remember Thy Creator in the Days of Thy Youth, While the Evil Days Come Not") which she had snatched up for pennies or had even been given by dealers. As with her past adventures (she had been the last person to see Thomas Merton before his death; she had marched with Martin Luther King; she had spent an afternoon with the Dalai Lama), this enterprise took on a romantic aura, and James wanted to be a part of it, even though he despised shopping in any form. And in any case, he never got to spend enough time with her.

A few weeks earlier, she had taken him to an antiques dealer on the highway. They wandered past phalanxes of tables, a thicket of lamps. James lacked the ability Melpomene had to lift the table or the lamp in her imagination and transport it to the dining room or the study, there by the window — no, next to the chair — and the fundamental disorientation that came over him whenever he saw furniture oddly juxtaposed, or lined up in military rows, or piled up willy-nilly, paralyzed him. When Melpomene spoke to him, he failed to hear her.

"Look!" she cried, shuffling through racks of moth-eaten velvet and taffeta ball gowns, her cheeks flushed. "We'll give a big party, and I'll wear one of these!"

He stopped, stock still, next to a kingly portrait of a Dalmatian posed against a backdrop of hills and rivers and forests, and drew in the oppressive breath of hundreds of lives brought together under one sagging roof: the smells of mildew and must and the honeyed, powdery aroma of old wood, the burning at the back of the throat caused by camphor.

The lips that had touched those scratched silver spoons with roses embedded in their bowls! The hands that had cradled that single blue Wedgwood cup! The limbs that patchwork quilt had warmed! On the flyleaf of *Eternity* by Maurice Maeterlinck was a bookplate: DANIEL AND SARAH BERNHEIM. In what solitary basement did the Saturday craftsman, perhaps listening to *Aïda* on the radio on a winter afternoon, turn those rabbit-shaped bookends on his lathe? And whose tarnished pewter baby porringer, with its stout handle and the monogram J? Could it have once been his own?

He gazed around in a panic. All of these objects had once belonged to individuals, and each of those owners had possessed an interior of some kind or another, and thoughts, and doubts, and they were hungry or sated, asleep or awake, and perhaps they had terrible fears of dying, fears of the thread that tied them to all their belongings being cut, of the objects flying out through space in all directions, moving on and on forever, their source long since dust.

The place was closing in on him. He went outside and inhaled deeply. He had to see the sky. The leafy crowns of the trees tossed in a breeze. Cars sped by. He vowed not to own anything and to get rid of the objects he had already. The world was senseless; his life had no significance whatsoever. After several minutes, he was gripped by loneliness.

He went inside and found Melpomene, his darling, his own, his only connection in this world. She held to her faith — in him and his perfectability, as well as in a Christ who was neither a bloodless concept nor the deity worshipped by most Christians but rather someone a little like herself, with a human body shot through· with a bright mystery whose source lay outside time and space. There she was, leaning over a dusty vitrine in which the sole display was an open case with a blue-velvet lining on which rested a finely worked gold chain with three baroque pearls. Her entire being filled his vision. Her expression was one of childlike rapture. Impossible to say what such a treasure was doing here. He wanted to buy it for her on the spot. Before she saw him, he hurried to the back, making china closets rattle, and whispered to the proprietor.

But had he understood her expression? For a long time she hadn't worn any jewelry — until this morning, as a matter of fact, when she had appeared with a gold band on her little finger. Yet she had stared at the pearls in the glass case the way the little match girl had stared through a window at the revelers feasting in warmth. And the ring? She explained that she had bought it from a desperate black man in front of the bus terminal. But hadn't she been wearing it the night James met her?

Gold became her. That night a few years ago at Ruth's, she had sat perfectly still, the candlelight at the dinner table making a pale sculpture of her face, a delicate chain at her throat giving off soft gleams as the links almost imperceptibly rose and fell. Her small, shapely hand rested on the handle of her knife, and if his memory was correct, the band just below the knuckle of her little finger. Her skin was smooth, her mouth serene and seductive. There she is, he thought. At last. He wanted a transcendent love. His marriage had been tentative for a long time; he had had adventures. Although during the evening she stayed near a thin, deeply tanned, exhausted-looking man with a shock of white hair who looked like a physicist but said he was "Kuno, the painter" and who seemed surprised that James didn't know his work or realize they were members of the same club, she flirted with James with heat and velocity, gazing up at him, wide-eyed, forming her mouth into a half kiss as she listened to him speak about Georges de La Tour, releasing a breathy laugh and exclaiming to the others, including James's wife, that James was brilliant. Melpomene's power, as she stood in the center of an admiring group, rapidly articulating the ethical problems of euthanasia, scared and aroused him. Later, when he telephoned her, she was always busy; she could talk just for a moment, and sometimes only in a whisper. She repeated that he was brilliant. Brilliant and good. Good possessed a particular meaning for her, one that he did not understand very well, even though, as she said, her job was to explain the good to people and to represent it. She never returned his calls.

One morning she phoned his house in the country and invited him to her apartment in the city — she was a visiting lecturer at a seminary then — and asked him to tell her all he knew concerning great paintings about marriage for a speech she would be giving to a convention of marital counselors. He understood from Ruth, Melpomene's oldest and closest friend, that Melpomene had her cadre of former lovers and would-be lovers. He did not want to take his place in their ranks; he had to keep hold of his brains; he had to think, and think with care. But within the hour he was on the train, passing under branches white with blossoms. It was enough that she admired him.

He had brought a book of Mauritius; she served him a delicious wine; she quoted verbatim from an article he had written about Notre-Dame and told him it was by far his best, as well as proof that he was subtle yet forceful, a pilgrim spirit like herself; she read him a poem by Andrew Marvell and smiled at him over the lines "Had we but world enough, and time"; and while they were listening to Bach's Chromatic Fantasy and Fugue, she began to massage his feet.

Just when he became comfortable with the expectation that they would see each other weekly, she no longer permitted him to visit and ordered him to remain forever with his wife. This proved insurmountable for him. And then she abruptly said she did not want to live if she could not live with him; she could no longer tolerate the life she had been leading, busy, celebrated, and alone. And then she happened to mention plans to move to a mountaintop retreat in California, or to Paris, or to Calcutta to work with Mother Teresa. She was afraid to go out alone after dark in the city; if only she had a safe haven near the sea, far away from everyone, she would give up her career and spend her days thinking, reading, walking; she would enter deeply into nature. At other times, he would embrace her and she would fiercely discard his arms and turn away, and all he wanted then was to shrivel up, and he would leave in silence. Eventually he realized that she didn't intend to harm him; she was absorbed in big questions, she struggled to live her philosophy, she was delicate, complex; he had to respect her need for solitude. A few days later he would ask to see her and she would blow in his ear, slide her hand down inside his waistband, and rush him into the bedroom, the whole time gazing intently into his eyes until he felt as if he were rising up, soaring, extraordinarily endowed, more potent than any man ever was or ever would be.

One day when they were about to go out for a picnic in the park, he found her sobbing. She refused to answer his questions. He held her.

"I'm sad," she said. "Very sad."

"Tell me, tell me!" he said, aching and alert, ready for action. Anything!

His shirtfront saturated with her tears, he listened to her confession. "You never have cared enough about me to give a single thought to marriage."

Baffled, he couldn't reply for several minutes, and his silence caused her to sob even harder. "Darling, darling! You said you had married enough already, that you didn't want that —"

"I never said such a thing! How could I? How could I? Oh, I'm too vulnerable — I let you inside, into the magic circle; I never should have done that. I'll be all right. I'll go away. I'll leave you alone."

"I am never letting you out of my sight again. You're the only woman for me." Later it seemed to him he had heard that line in a movie. No matter. They spent the rest of the day making love, and she showed skills that he had imagined her too innocent to possess.

Aroused, full of longing for her touch, her mouth (tonight, the promise of tonight!), as if she were thousands of miles away rather than a few yards, he set the table, choosing two plates and two cups that were replicas of dishes which he had seen in a Claesz still life of oysters and lemons in the Rijksmuseum and had found the same day in an antiques shop nearby. He brought the thin-walled china back as a gift to her before their marriage.

He would admit to her his uneasiness, speak of the need for more soundproofing in the study; she would dismiss his jealousy and reassure him. I even went so far as to take this stupid shell out of your drawer, he would say. They would laugh. His trust would return. And tonight, in bed . . .

Dearest . . . still love . . . The sun went under the clouds that were blowing down from the north. The room dimmed. Shadows disappeared, bringing a thrill of relief and anticipation. Something was going to happen. An eclipse. An earthquake. His work would have to be postponed. When his fingers had touched the shell under the panties, he had jumped. But it was just calcium carbonate, easily crushed in his palm if he chose. Women did things like that — kept desiccated roses and seashells and hid them around.

And her arrangements didn't concern him: he could scarcely keep up with all that she did, with the people she saw. She could have been saving someone's life when he overheard her. Even a stray dog had once prompted an outpouring of her solicitude, and her subsequent talk began with the story of how she had taken in the wretched creature, its fur ridden with swollen ticks, its hind leg scraped and bleeding, and bathed it and bandaged it and found it a home. The fellowship was obviously moved. "Let's try to remember Christ's injunction: 'Inasmuch as ye have done it unto the least of these my brethren, ye have done it unto me.' "

Perhaps she'd been forced to whisper on the phone because she was preparing a surprise for him, or perhaps she had been reassuring some forlorn soul. She felt love and compassion for all the needy seekers who crowded around her, and she gave them her full attention. A mystery to him; he didn't care about humanity in general, and at church functions, when people regarded him with adoration as well, he felt, lapped as he was by the overflow, acute chagrin. He was neither good nor brilliant.

He placed a wedge of pale cheese on a carving board. He washed three big pears with stippled skins. They were not pears from the dwarf trees in the garden; those were small and bitter. He filled a little basket with walnuts and searched out the nutcracker, softly opening and closing cabinets. He did all this with concentration, to use up the time.

Seven miles above the earth, a glint. It made a roaring wind. In the interior of the glint, someone kicked the back of Kuno's seat. He kept his elbows tucked in to avoid touching the passengers on either side. On a sketch pad he made desultory pencil marks: a mouth, an eye; hers. He looked down at the shifting line between water and land until a cloud intervened.

Away from Melpomene, he had been much more placid; he found himself happy thinking about her while spending his time with other women. But in the Orangerie, standing before a Soutine portrait of a woman whose face was a violent mass with desperate, smeared eyes, he became tearful and dazed, nearly losing consciousness.

Who else was like her? Who else so much like him? His painting had become energetic and remarkable after he fell in love with her; she declared him a genius; she sent him away; she called him back; she said she could not live without him and then married someone else, that pedant, that empty Savile Row suit. Kuno went off to work in Paris, to make connections with a gallery there, but he did nothing. Wandered around France and Italy. Melpomene's sunny replies only drove him deeper into his yearning. He began a correspondence with Ruth and got the real story from her. Melpomene was suffering: she cried for hours; for days at a stretch she was unable to sleep; she was going to leave husband, church, everything. Disappear.

He swallowed. His mouth was dry; there was no hope of help, here in the sky. Half an hour more to go. He balanced his pad on his knee and began a new sketch, just to have something to show her. He had barely been able to hear her voice, even though he had jammed the receiver against his ear. Perhaps she would be gone before he could get to her.

As she played back the morning's messages on her answering machine, she saw in the mirror her own eyes. If only they were grayer, like the eyes of that woman of Kuno's; *her* eyes were a striking gray, thickly rimmed with black — such vanity! Melpomene had never needed makeup herself.

("Damn your eyes," Patrick, the Irish poet, had exclaimed. Melpomene was eighteen at the time; with her dark hair falling straight to her waist, and her high cheekbones, she resembled, people said, an Indian princess.) She stepped back. The skin under her chin appeared loose, the beginning of a wattle. Like her mother! No, it was just the position of her head; if she lengthened her neck, the extra flesh disappeared. ("Hi?" murmured a voice on the machine. "This is Kristen. . . . I'm sorry. . . . I need to tell you something.") Her stomach — she forced it against her spine. The new dress would conceal her weight. She really ought to exercise. Kuno used to nag her about that. He wanted her to be healthy. He, at least, had wanted her to live and had brought her fresh juices and ordered fruit sent. He wore himself out at the gym, on the running track, in his scull. But she had no time. She had to work. She was poor, a poor pastor. ("Marty Furman calling about your tax projections for next year," the machine said.) She had no one she could truly depend upon; she had to fight or starve. But in the warm, humid room created by Kuno's desiring gaze, she became beautiful, alluring, rich.

Even his flaws endeared him to her; they weren't real flaws; just quirks. ("Hi? This is Kristen? I left a message earlier. May I please have another appointment right away if it's not too much trouble?") He had appealed to her for help. She would give it. Together they would work on his lapses. Together, using truth. Truth — it was all that mattered, finally. In medical school, when she had taken care of the dying, and seen them toss away their masks in exhaustion and begin to live just at the last moment, the falseness, the lies, the mechanicalness of those who consider themselves among the living came into sharp focus for her. What was the solution? She found the answer on a visit to Notre-Dame. She returned home with her vocation. Truth, relentless truth. (Men loved that — her ideals.) She would help him understand; she would again make the effort to change him. With her, he would realize his potential as the most gifted of artists, the most sensitive of souls, the soundest of businessmen. His portrait of her could perhaps have been more beautiful, the mouth less tough, with its little row of sharp teeth and heavily impastoed lips, but he had sold it for $100,000, a fact unknown even to his wife (he was still married then). But above all, he was the most masterful of lovers — even ferocious. She yielded; he tormented her, a little. You would not suspect it: he was small-boned and slight. But a man, a real man! What passion! And the body of a youth. She could barely stand it. The more ardent her sensations, the shyer she became. Although people reported to her the most intimate and shocking scenes, and she received them with a neutral grace, she herself could never describe such details about herself to anyone. (Who did she have to confide in, really? Ruth was scarcely an equal.) When she was not in control (she said to the gray-eyed, long-necked woman in the mirror), she felt a profound embarrassment, and kept her head down, and turned away. Men found this enchanting and disconcerting. In trembling voices, they told her she was fragile and needed to be cared for. The idea of marriage would promptly take shape in her brain, even as she was asking herself why she should alter her life for someone who happened to make her body experience particular sensations. But what was feral must be domesticated; what was accidental must be perfected. And she wanted more. She wanted a vow; she wanted a man to swear in front of everyone that he celebrated her, that he prized her above all else, that he was proud of her, that he would protect her. (So that everyone would know that she was not a cause for shame, that she was not a huge nothing.) And any man who would not do that had failed at love.

Love — she was so weary of it. No one seemed to talk about anything else, at least to her (even Suzanne and Kristen, who ought to focus just on survival), and Melpomene's own heavy chain of deliberations on the subject did not make her ultimately happy. No, the thoughts that arose from desire never took satisfactory shape in the external world; there was always a terrible gulf between the wish and the object (he had called from the air, but he had not satisfied her passion), and besides, those thoughts were a narcotic, and she did not want to fall asleep. Her true joy lay in being clear-witted, in working, helping others, taking walks, listening to music, reading, keeping each day in quiet order so that time was somehow beautifully used and preserved. Right now, she swore, she would follow her true joy and forget everything else. From now on she would conduct herself perfectly.

Never again would she permit these cyclones of discontent to overtake her; she would give up impatience and disappointment; she would never again choose what was bound to make her miserable. Her poet husband had said, "Love, you are forever weaving your own shroud." Perhaps she had surrounded herself with the wrong people from the beginning, in every city, in every congregation, throughout her schooling . . . because of distortions originating with her parents. Or perhaps her refined alertness was to blame, her keen and lonely perception of the world. Consciousness. The terrible virus of consciousness! A good topic for a talk. But to blame was to lie. From this second on, she would take complete responsibility. Whatever the source of these black notions, she would combat them with all her strength — and no one was more valiant; she was in her prime.

"Kuno here." The trees in the hedgerow shook. *Kuno here.* The woman in the mirror reddened and lowered her head. Oh.

"I've just gone through customs. I'll call you when I get home. Please, please wait for me, my sweet Mel."

From childhood she had always imagined that the birds perched in the tree of life had found sanctuary there. But perhaps they were preparing to fly away.

Her hand shaking, she jabbed a button that reversed time: she returned to the moment when he had called her. The connection crackled. He had phoned as soon as he'd gotten off the plane; that was good. Twice in one day he had called. And he would call her again, he'd said he would. He had asked her to wait. Oh, God. How long would it take him to reach home? She listened again to the message. The timbre of his voice: flat, perhaps melancholy? A trace of contrition? Yes, her bones would be mingled with his in the grave; she knew that for certain; they were as one. Oh, she murmured again. He was back. The room became shabby and empty.

Five

IN THE LIVING ROOM he sat with the headphones on and listened to the Impromptu again and again. During the fourth playing he heard Schubert's voice, full, wordless, impelling, announcing what it was like to be Schubert, gifted, mortal, alone. During the seventh playing, James simply heard the music. During the twelfth, he became the music.

She would smile when she saw the table spread in the light — the shapely green pears, the yellow slab of cheese, the fresh walnuts, the two plates and cups with their faint opalescence. Nothing had happened, everything was all right. He had misinterpreted. The seashell must be returned before she noticed. He should never have been eavesdropping in the first place.

He would tell her about Schubert, and she would ask him how the book was going. I've been doing a lot of contemplating, he would say. Organizing things in my mind. She might then cock her head in a gentle reproach, as if to reply: Yes, but that's all you do. When will you start to work? But he would insist on the importance of the thoughts with which he had awakened today. O world, thou was the forest, etc. And you are the forest to this hart. He would kiss her on the mouth and squeeze her hips, and slide his hands over her buttocks; as in the old days, he would ask if she were free tonight.

But she might refuse him. He cracked a walnut and examined the convoluted folds of the nutmeat. Under his breath he whistled the slow part of the Impromptu. (The mountaineer could not go on; he would never reach the summit; he would only hear the ocean rolling far below; Schubert knew he hadn't long to live when he wrote this.) When Melpomene had chosen James, he had been relieved as well as surprised. Unlike most of the women he had known, she was independent and definite about her goals. She decided she would buy a new car and did so; she knew that on a particular Wednesday next June she would be delivering the commencement address at a liberal arts college in New Hampshire; she determined that it would take her a year to read the complete works of Wittgenstein and, as far as he was aware, she was now making her way through the *Philosophical Investigations*. In German. People came to call on her on Tuesday, Friday, and Saturday; on Friday and Saturday between visitors, she wrote her lecture; on alternate Sundays, after the service, she presided over the philosophy-group luncheon. She could converse adroitly about any subject, and she had a splendid mouth and hands. She had been surrounded by men when he met her, and yet she now declared to James twice a day that she loved him. He had thought, transformed by her breath in his ear, Now she will arrange everything; I am free. He popped the nutmeat into his mouth.

He was immensely privileged. His awe, since youth, that any woman would let him make love to her, that she would submit to such an unbelievable and intimate deed, was enormous. Melpomene had subsequently wanted him to pledge, in the presence of a crowd of people, most of whom neither of them particularly liked, that she was everything to him; otherwise they could not go on together. Their trysts, the secrecy, the hiding, excited him — the danger. And having just signed papers finishing his old marriage, he was not eager to sign any more for a while, and he didn't understand her urgency. She said, with absolute conviction, "If you don't want to marry me in three weeks, if you can't decide by then, it means you don't love me, and I love you too much to let you hurt me in this way." She would be forced, in the name of truth, to leave him forever; she would just go away and not trouble him further; how could he claim to love her and yet delay attesting to the permanence and the seriousness of their bond? Was he ashamed of marrying a minister?

He took two clean napkins from a drawer. He sat at the table and put a pear on his plate and listened to a quail whistling on the lawn and the high-speed gibberish of Melpomene's answering machine being rewound again and again.

She appeared in the kitchen doorway, frowning.

"Here's lunch," James said. Where was her smile? Didn't she see his still life on the table before her? "Special treat."

She squinted in the sunshine as if she had a headache. "That's a pretty skirt." It was a confusion of dark leaves and flowers, like the shaded part of the hedgerow in late summer or early fall. "Is it new?" He brushed a piece of lint from the fabric.

"This? Poor box."

"Poor box! Really, darling, you don't have to —"

"Oh, don't worry. It's a donation from this incredibly rich woman over on Alewife Road who isn't even in the fellowship. She'll never know, and I gave her a big receipt for her taxes. Anyway, I'm not rich, James." She went to the bay window and then turned and approached the table and cleared her throat. Her lower lip began to tremble. She began to breathe erratically. "Mother — mother called again. She's in bad shape. She really wants me to come."

"Oh, no! Do you think she's really that serious?" Surely Melpomene was telling him the truth; he flushed.

The trembling stopped. "Probably she's just hysterical. Another one of her ploys." The trembling resumed and captured her voice as well as her chin. "But I'm very afraid; I'm very worried this time." Her eyes filled with tears.

She had often asked James to accompany her on visits to her mother. Protect me, Melpomene would say to him. Just hold me.

He got up and put his arms around her. To allay her hurts gave him a reason to live. What did he have to fear? Happiness made his throat constrict as it had in the night when he thought of her form next to his. "I'll drive you up immediately."

She drew back. "That's sweet of you. You're so good. But I can run up there — or I might even fly. Ah, there's Kristen's car —"

James glanced out at the drive. "But it's lunchtime. You promised —"

"It's an emergency. She's desperate."

"She can wait ten minutes while you sit down and eat. You didn't have breakfast. You promised me you wouldn't do this anymore. You asked me to make certain you didn't."

She returned to the window and kept her face concealed. (Kristen floated, with an eerie smile, toward the waiting room door.) Who was he to drown her in admonitions? She had to be slender, for Kuno. Why did James presume to crowd her, to intrude upon her, when he himself stood before her in a disgusting old sweatshirt, a pathetic heap, incapable of a few moments of honest work or real passion? But now she was getting nettled. Enough. No reason to lose control. Kuno had called. It was important to maintain tranquillity, because when she was tranquil, she was beautiful (James had told her that, unwittingly consoling her when Kuno had deserted her). But James was intolerable, really. What woman could endure his nattering, his lint-picking? Even Ruth, stupid enough to tolerate her dreary husband, would be put to the test with James. Yes, Melpomene was justified in wanting to run away, because — Oh, there was the oak with its flaming crown, and the enameled blue sky backlighting it. She had made her vow to prevent the darkness from welling up.

"I'm only saying this because I'm concerned about you," he said. "Please."

Why was he trying to frighten her? Always that belittling tone. So overbearing! And his face, horrible, about to writhe. Did he really want to upset her? At any moment she could stop thinking in this way. She was the producer and the heroine; the film had begun running long ago, noble and certain. No one comprehended how hard she had to struggle; she ministered to everyone and no one ministered to her. Yes, if she wanted to, she could think in this small-minded way: she no longer lived alone, and yet here she was, waking up weeping, just as in the old days. He no longer needed her. He scarcely could glance at her as he made his pronouncements; she might as well be a table or a bed. Of course, that was how it always happened. She had given him everything — what other woman would do that for him? He had refused her. She had to protect herself. She had had to overcome tremendous hardships: her parents had treated her like a talking doll for display at parties; her work and worries were so demanding that she sometimes felt she could not — Enough. She could start to fall right now if she were not an alert and developed individual, if, like those around her, she were oblivious to her own processes. But such attributions were petty, and she was not petty. The worst thing about women, their pettiness. Despicable, really. So she would say yes to everything. She would overlook his lapses. Small, really, when she considered how kind he was. Today was new. Kuno had called twice.

James took a step toward her and reached for her hand.

A swell of revulsion overcame her. She threw his hand down and batted at the air. "Get away from me!" she whispered hoarsely, and bolted down the hall. Then she made a half turn and added, quietly, so that Kristen would not overhear, "Oh, I'm sorry, dear, I didn't mean that. It's just that the thing with Mother . . ."

Again she hurried away, and her study door closed. He heard her voice, musical and hearty: "Hello, Kristen, dear!"

When Melpomene went without food or sleep for even a

short time, she became touchy, and then morose. If he told her to eat she said she was too fat, and if he told her to rest she said it was bad to be lazy. She did not dare sleep, because she had to take care of others, to earn enough so that she would not starve. She was deaf to his reassurances, and when he pointed out how much she had in the bank under her own name, she said it would not be enough to take care of her in her old age. He sliced a pear and licked the juice from his fingers. She was giving him a terrible message today, but he could not follow it. He saw only bits. Maybe she actually was distraught about her mother. But her interest in the old woman (whom she had wished aloud to be dead more than once) seemed too abrupt. On the other hand, if she were planning to meet a lover, there were a dozen better excuses available.

The flesh of the pear was perfumed and grainy, the cheese, hard and salty, the walnuts, a little bitter. He ate quickly, scarcely aware after the first few bites. The waters of the bay cast a field of rippling brilliance on the ceiling. Light turned up in odd places. Mauritius demonstrated that very well in his paintings, whose verisimilitude made them border on the surreal.

The horizon was the goal. Kristen stared out the window. She searched for the means to make the Reverend understand that the field had recently been under the ocean, and the ocean had been in the air, and before that, the air had been in pieces of matter flung through space, and those pieces, not so long ago, had been contained in a lone particle and before the particle —

"Kristen, dear?"

At last she found it. Language, whose shivering bursts had come from thought, which had arisen from matter, which had exploded out of a singularity: "I don't want anything to change."

"Why do you say that?"

The boughs felt the passage of wings (the electricity in her nerves) and quivered, and in the roots the joyful tremors passed into the earth, which contained the dead and the seeds in which were inscribed the history and future of trees. She had returned to Gabriel's house. Without his arms around her, she would not survive this chaos. He had sent her back to the Reverend.

A bang came from another room, startling Kristen. Her eyes grew wide, and she lifted her arms, her fingers splayed. "What was that?"

"Just a door closing. Don't worry." Melpomene had spoken to James about keeping quiet. But of course he did not care. Let him ruin the calm needed by this poor, disturbed girl. Let her waste her time and Melpomene's inquiring about slammed cabinet doors. What did it matter to him? She was right to go to Kuno. With James she had believed that at last she had found someone predictable, someone for whom she was the center, someone who would sustain her, with whom (if it wasn't too late) she could even try at last to have a child; but now it was obvious that he would not sacrifice one second for her. His books, his headphones, his so-called work, always came first. Not a trace of sympathy for her about Mother, and Melpomene could kill herself, too, as long as his precious meals weren't interrupted. She would have liked, just for once, just for a moment, just for the time it took one match to burn, to come first with another person.

Kristen sniffed and blinked. The sharp crack that had rent the veil of the air was the sign. The woman across from her, inhaling and exhaling, making it day then night then day then night, had folded her hands, and a shaft of sun now struck her womb, confirming that all was finished. The door had closed. "You're the horizon, and I'm disappearing."

"Disappearing? But you're right here, dear." Disappearing — ah, Melpomene knew this very well; the void, waiting right there under all the layers of sights and sounds and thoughts. Even though she did not come first with Kuno either, she was the only person who truly loved him. He was alone, no matter what other woman he was with. Melpomene held his life — he was nothing without her. She had it in writing, in his thick-nibbed, slanting hand, in the letter in her skirt pocket. "Kristen, just focus on being here. Collect yourself. Here, look at me. You see? Here we are, together."

The smell of fried clams in the gloomy restaurant had made Melpomene queasy. Kuno took her out to the parking lot. Water sloshed against pilings. He jangled coins in the pocket of his windbreaker. She observed herself, and she observed him. She felt she was balancing on a slender rod, and as long as she remained relaxed and her eyes remained fastened on his, she would get to the other side. The sea slid up the horizon and fell; if only she could travel away, to the horizon. She tried to make him feel better about the terrible blow he was delivering. She congratulated herself: she did not collapse on the gravel and weep and hold his ankles and plead. He pulled a scallop shell out of his pocket and told her he had selected it with care, adding that of course he could not risk giving her anything that would make James suspicious. She took satisfaction in the fleeting resentment Kuno allowed himself to show when he pronounced the name of his rival. Kuno had given her the gold ring for her little finger at the beginning, and a bouquet of red rosebuds on an afternoon when, after she had banished him forever, he returned and demanded to be let in or he would kick the door down. He had not let her speak, and only kissed her, and their love that day had reached a pinnacle; intolerable. And then, at the end, the shell. An inexpensive out. He had never understood that she wanted nothing, nothing, nothing from him — unlike his wife, unlike the new woman. But she lied: she wanted everything.

Kristen's big, pure eyes remained on Melpomene, who couldn't bear to be looked at like that for so long. She crinkled her face into a patient smile. "So, Kristen, you see? We're here, safe, together."

"I, I just wanted to say how important you've been to me."

Kuno had asked her in his message to wait; then they really would meet. Her heart began to beat with a harshness that made her start. She spread her hands in her lap. But there was Kristen, watching her expectantly; oh, terrible, this self-absorption. She ought to be ashamed. "Yes, dear. And you mean a lot to me. You were the first person to come to see me here."

Kristen twisted the hem of her skirt between her fingers. "The glue is gone."

"The glue is gone?" A panel of sunlight moved over Melpomene's lap. The backs of her hands, mottled with brown spots and webbed with fine lines she did not recall seeing before, seemed unfamiliar. An expensive skin cream would solve the problem, but she should have started using one years ago, when she was still an impoverished medical student. Of course she had to go without food in those days, and cosmetics would have been her last thought. And after deciding to become a minister, she had to subsist on tea and toast, somehow supporting her studies at the seminary by frantically toiling at any job she could find. Her father opposed her marriage to the poet and then insisted she conceal her divorce, and would not help her. (She had vowed never again to depend on anyone.) Now she could afford an expensive cream, but she had no time. She was forced to scurry about doing charitable acts, to perform before a group of half-asleep infants, and to sit in a dismal room and listen to the minutiae of their lives. All the garbage and shit they were ashamed to reveal to psychiatrists with fancy diplomas, who were paid lavishly for their time, these feeble creatures brought to her, the final refuge, and assumed that she would receive them gratis as Christ received the weak and heavy-laden. While she labored alone, her hands had aged and all around her, in other rooms, people were laughing in easy camaraderie and loafing and feasting. "Kristen, why is it that you keep looking at me like that?"

Against the mother's breast Kristen could rest; in her lap Kristen could sleep. "I don't dare close my eyes." And you know, Kristen said silently, sending the picture through the air to the Reverend's brain, that you are the axis of the world, immobile and everlasting.

"Why is that?"

"I start to dream, and the dreams are worse than being awake. When I'm awake at least I don't disappear."

"Disappear? Why do you keep talking about disappearing?"

What a good idea, to go away, far away, far away from

betrayals. Kuno: erotic, intelligent, firm, generous (she moved her fingers slightly to mark each quality). And yet he'd behaved in a stupid, weak, miserly fashion. He had betrayed her again and again, and, perversely, her desire only grew. (She was beyond hunger now. A vein in her scalp began to throb.) Kuno and she had agreed on a wedding date (or anyway, she wrote one down in her book). Fortunately, James had already begun pursuing her when Kuno came up with implausible reasons for postponement (he was about to start a new phase in his painting and needed to retreat; he wanted to earn enough so that she could retire). James, with his money, his social connections, and his professional reputation, brought out Kuno's dueling instincts and for a while rekindled his passion for Melpomene. But he would not give up the other woman, not even when Melpomene threatened to marry James. Besides, she was becoming fond of James's quiet attentions; he was timid, but she would build him up; he was intellectual, and pleased to make love to her all the time. Mature, sensible companionship: that was what she wanted, rather than these childish fluctuations and ambivalences. And even James could become masterful if she caressed him and whispered to him enough. But how much time did she have? Her hands — claws; she couldn't look at them. And a balloon was expanding inside her skull.

Kristen sighed and extended her arms and lay them on the back of the sofa. A great warm wave swept over her. It was finished. She had heard the crack of doom. And she was not crazy — the Reverend had heard it, too. The birds perched close to the spine of the tree of life; on each branch, one bird looked on while its companion ate the fruit. No longer afraid, expanding, prepared for the sacrifice, she spoke. "Time is a substance. It grinds everything down. Everything disappears."

Melpomene inclined her head toward Kristen and looked at her for a while in silence.

The silence confirmed the walls, the trees, the sky, the ground, in their revulsion of the two-legged thing that called itself Kristen; but she was all right. The horizon retreated to a vast distance; the journey would be long.

Melpomene would take prompt action: calls to the family; medication; hospitalization. The phone rang softly, and the answering machine clicked on. The waiting had to be over now. The instant Kristen left, Melpomene would check her machine and then call the psychiatrist who always responded to these problem cases. "I won't disappear, dear, and neither will you. I'll be here. Now you need to go, go and rest."

Kristen did not move. The Reverend, too, had incorporated time into her flesh. It filled Kristen with anguish to see the dead parts of a living face, the stone blended cunningly with the flesh; horrible —

The Reverend, agitated in the light of Kristen's gaze because she must sense what had befallen her own face, took Kristen's hand and helped her up. "My dear, you need your rest. Now go. I want you to go home — home, not to Gabriel's — and eat a nice lunch. You need nourishment — and I want you to get into bed, and close your eyes, and rest and rest."

If only I could have what I give, thought Melpomene. Two bodies in a room, breathing. Sometimes that was enough.

Six

NO, JAMES DECIDED, she wasn't going to come out of
her study. She preferred to remain there with another murmuring voice. In fact, she would keep the other murmuring
voice there as long as she could. It was selfish of him to
demand her time; anyway, if he importuned her now, she
might refuse him tonight. Quietly, he searched through the
cabinets for a taste of something sweet. A cupboard door
made a loud click when he closed it, and so he left the
remaining doors ajar. He refilled his coffee cup and softly
climbed the stairs, silently whistling the Impromptu, which
remained in his throat like an unvoiced call.

Without seating himself, he began to type at the computer. Dearest Alice. No voices came from below now.
Dearest, dearest Alice. But he did not print out the letter —
long, sincere, erupting with treacherous notions he had no
idea he possessed, spilling over with heat; it remained en-
coded in pulses of yes and no, saved inside the metal box.

Alice. He had been in some sort of building with pictures on the wall and he had gone inside paintings, had escaped with utter happiness into the fresh, immortal world, and then Alice had appeared and they had embraced, and the embrace was of a cell-penetrating intensity he had never felt in his waking life and yet was utterly familiar, and now he was here in this room, on this planet (its sky, arching over the clouds residing in the light-doubling mirror, was still bright), and all around stretched the endless vacuum and absolute cold of space, but Alice at this hour might be getting out of her bath, her flesh wet and very warm, and she might at this instant, as she reached for a towel and rubbed it along her strong, tanned thigh, remember him.

His coffee was cold. He sat down stiffly. His knee hurt. Could it be arthritis? Was he already old enough for that? Alice! My God, he thought, I loved her. And I didn't even know it. Was it too late? He had to work now, he had vowed to begin today. But later he would finish the letter.

Opening a big book of hand-tipped reproductions in muted, rich colors, he turned to *Woman Weighing Gold,* James's strongest evidence for his case. Her face was as pristine and composed as a Madonna's; her head was slightly tilted as if she were regarding the Babe rather than the gold scale, which was suspended from the pinch of her thumb and forefinger and which was so delicate it was almost invisible; behind her, in a painting of the Last Judgment, Christ, in an oval of light, floated above the saved and the damned; before her stood a table half-covered with a Persian carpet of a geometric design in ocher, blue, and rust which resembled the carpet Melpomene had found for this room, and on the table, next to a pair of calipers, rested a mirror, a sliver with an opaque sheen. Beyond the book, the window framed heaving cedar boughs and racing clouds. The weather was changing.

Here he would begin. On another day, he would dutifully set out the commonplaces, which no one would bother to read and which were far removed from the experience of actually looking at and absorbing a work of art, but which, according to some dread rule, had always to be presented at length, with footnotes. On another day he would write about the scales in which Thoth weighed human hearts at the threshold of the Egyptian hereafter; about De Hooch's *Gold Weigher;* about Vermeer's *A Woman Holding a Balance,* with its nearly identical but somewhat starker composition (a copy that Vermeer must have made during his apprenticeship; what better way to learn that technique is not sufficient, that one must have something to say as well?). But today James would leap over the history and take on the painting as he had taken on the Schubert Impromptu; he would only gaze, empty, ready; and another time he would speak of the jewels on the table representing vanity, and the mirror, the search for self-knowledge, and the scales, the opportunity to choose between heaven and hell, and the Last Judgment, a reminder of the consequences of all our earthly acts (whatever we do goes on happening forever). At the moment, his other self was calling from behind the clouded glass, making mysterious movements. Why did Mauritius care enough about this scene to devote himself so completely to it, to spend all he had, to imbue every square inch with an intelligible light?

To say the woman was regarding her own soul and weighing it would invite ridicule these days, when any inquiry that went beyond pigment analysis or sociological speculation or discussion of allegory might provoke scorn. And this absurd idea (he would never put it on paper) of the other self, waiting to receive the consciousness of the artist, creating a field of attraction between the painting and his brain! Nevertheless, his fingers moved over the lettered and numbered keys, and his ruminations became glimmering patterns on the screen.

A gold chain and a string of pearls spilled out from a casket. A gold ring, almost invisible, rested on a fold in the carpet. The intimate glow of Mauritius's thought slipped in through a closed curtain and enveloped the room (this painting and *The Instruction of the Virgin* were the two dark Mauritiuses; their dim, rosy ambiance was that of the interior of the womb or the inside of an eyelid). The woman waited for the balance to stop quivering, all her attention serenely gathered on her task. If she was impatient, the quivering would never stop. She had only to wait: that was her work. She ignored the spilling pearls, the gold ring. The supple light touched her pale forehead, and at her back, in obscurity, Christ sent souls to heaven or to hell. At the Rijksmuseum, James had arranged to examine the painting with a microscope, and had discovered that the two gold pans, each composed of a single fine and masterly brush-stroke, were empty. What was Mauritius saying, then? Was the woman weighing, with absolute composure — with all her being gracefully bent toward — nothing?

The hawk circled; shadows lengthened; the wind droned; his stomach, judging exactly which chemicals were needed, digested his lunch. But he remained contentedly in a room in seventeenth-century Delft. He barely breathed, so hopeful was he that the balance would come to rest and that he would be saved.

All the cabinet doors had been thrown open so that she would hurt her aching head. On the table, one plate and one cup —the wastefully expensive ones James had given her; she could not look at them without exasperation. One napkin, from a set of new ones she was saving. One pear, a bit of malodorous cheese, some nuts. An obvious insult. Where was her toasted muffin, her glass of milk?

For hours and hours now she had been waiting. Oh, years. She saw herself, heard her thoughts, carried around her person, this person, not some other person. But this person happened to be unbearable, and her punishment was never to be able to rest from herself. Gravity was pulling her down, bending her bones. The glare through the dark cedars stung her eyes. She had to defend herself from such terrible treatment.

Where was James? He was scarcely innocent; her thigh had a hideous bruise. If he had abandoned her, he must have gone on foot, or some woman had picked him up; his car remained next to hers in the drive. (But of course James would not leave her; this was just a story she had invented. She felt this way only because she was so exhausted, so hungry, because — oh, never mind. Excuses, and her curse was always to know the truth.)

All right, then: analyze what you feel. Above all, be objective. While she was with Kristen, Kuno had called from his apartment and left a message saying he wasn't sure when he could see her. Soon, though. When she called him back, there was no answer. He was quite aware that she was waiting to hear from him, that she needed to talk to him, to

arrange things, confirm the reservations at the inn and so
on. He knew that she would often be unable to answer the
phone. Did he think that a brief call from him was all it took
to bring her trotting back? After Kristen had finally dragged
herself out the door, Melpomene immediately phoned him,
only to hear a recording of his voice, an imitation Kuno,
nauseatingly courteous. It was all right. That was Kuno.
She must not invent. Of course he couldn't help abrading
her. But after so long she had still not acquired calluses; if
anything, she had become more sensitive, while the happy
herd with their tough hides thundered and blundered over
her. The laws of the herd were not the laws of Melpomene
Gilman. The Reverend Melpomene Gilman. Kuno thought
he could treat her like any woman. But it was all right. She
would be fine. She had a great deal to do. And if James chose
this time to fling all the cabinets open and forget about their
lunch and disappear after the enormous sacrifices she had
made for him, well, then, that was James. A great soul could
encompass whatever came its way, and she fervently wanted
her soul to be great. She could forgive.

But ought she to forgive what they were doing to her?
The violence? She couldn't take any more of their violence;
she was frail; her health might go at any minute; this life was
killing her. (But really that was not the case, because she had
awakened happy, she loved everyone, the bay, the garden,
the flaming crown of the oak, and this afternoon Gabriel
Porter, who was a famous musician, had an appointment to
see her, and she was wearing an expensive blouse and
custom-made shoes, and she was important to society, representing the good, encouraging right conduct.)

But they were trying to push her to the bottom of the sea.
She had to claw and thrash with all her might. She was right

to be distrustful; the proof flashed out from the dent in the fender of her car, right out there in the drive. Her own terrible stench rose around her; she was soaked in her own evil fluids. She had no time; she had to struggle to stay alive, just to stay alive, and her husband, one more in the series, had abandoned her, leaving a cup, a plate, a piece of rotten fruit, and *he* had abandoned her. An immense swelling pressure poured into the room, pumping up the interior of her skull and pounding through her blood vessels. She bit the inside of her wrist.

Dialing the phone with trembling fingers, she made a reservation for a one-way flight to Paris, for that very night. No one would be able to locate her. She would find peace in a little hotel room, anonymous, far from the rage.

Clouds raced past the sun. Diagonal flares flickered out and lit up, flickered out and lit up. Silver darts shot out of the cup and the plate. She had no time, and the danger was coming. Order was what was needed; she would work until she dropped; alone, she would fend off the catastrophe. No one cared about her.

She had to avoid the wall sockets, the electrical appliances, the glittering knives. She dropped the pear in the garbage, and the cup cracked in half in the sink, bang!

She didn't do it; it was certainly not her action that broke the cup; her moves were always careful and attentive; she wanted to perform every task perfectly; these bad things just happened to her. Reflections snaked along polished metal, causing the plate to smash on the floor. She had to hurry. The frightening thing was about to unleash its force. She ran.

*

He scrutinized the graceful circle made by the thumb and forefinger of the woman. In those bones was recorded the evolution of the human hand, the development of the opposable thumb from which all of civilization was suspended. He touched his own thumb; he had been carrying that same information around in his body since conception. Suppose the painting celebrated the opposable thumb and its manifold productions — the delicate scale, the mirror, the string of pearls, the finely worked gold ring, heaven, hell, nothingness.

The door opened with a sharp crack. He jumped. Melpomene stood on the threshold.

Smelling the tang of her perfume, he forgot that she had pushed him away an hour or two ago, that she might love any given man more than she loved him. Delighted by her visit, he grinned and pointed to the picture in the open book, to the geometric carpet that resembled the Heriz on the floor.

She remained in the doorway, hunched, pale, silent, chest heaving, hands hanging at her sides. For an instant, she, too, forgot, and was replaced by an earlier Melpomene who was simply glad to see that he was there, alive, his expression rapt, his work before him — just what she had wished for him all this time. But then the Melpomene of the present moment conquered her predecessor, and the force surged up, the pressure again ballooned in her skull, and all the horrors they — *they* — had committed against her rushed in; just let him, him, the worst of the perpetrators, dare to smile!

He rose halfway out of his chair. "Darling, what is it?"

The face — not her face; impossible — was fragmented,

and slashed with furrows. Her lips drew back from her teeth. One eyebrow shot up and the opposite corner of her mouth dragged itself down. She tried to speak and failed.

"What?" His shoulders tightened, and he compressed his neck and drew in his head.

The separate parts of her face began to cohere, and the mask hardened into the expression of the prisoner who has resolved never to yield to tortures. "You. You. Some lunch together! I even postponed an appointment." This was not true, but in the instant it seemed true, and after a moment or two, even to the Melpomene who was watching the furious Melpomene, it became absolutely, irrevocably true, and the details — her datebook with the midday name crossed off, the dismay in the voice of the person (Ellen, Ellen Brent it was) on the other end of the line, Melpomene's firm trust in her hope that she and James would at last have a chance to sit down alone together and enjoy a meal, her generosity in taking the time to prepare some food he liked — immediately cemented themselves to the assertion and gave it unshakable support. "And this is how you treat — how you treat — how you treat someone, someone whose mother — whose mother may already have killed herself."

Slowly he pulled himself away from the green rows of letters on the screen, away from the woman waiting for the scales to stop trembling; he would never again look on this vision he had thought was his life. The powerful current that would take him away was already flowing, but he clung to the interval before the door had opened. And while Melpomene, white and shaking, kept her fingers splayed by her sides, and James's hand continued to rest on the corner of the page, and his tongue lay parched in his mouth, and his

voice was unable to work, the knowledge in his bones remained, always with him and always hidden from him.

"Yes, suicide! And I didn't know where you were, and if
you want to run around with some, some — well, it's nothing to me. You're free to — to do whatever you like. I know
you think I'm lying, and what if I am? It's because you force
me to. Go, go — go do — go do whatever you like!"

"What?" He felt himself being jerked up as if by the roots
of his hair. He did not have an explanation for her, but he
would create one. He would make her tranquil. To stop her
from injuring her eternity (there it was, right there in the
painting; look!), he would apologize. Atone. Anything to
end his fear. His hands shook. "I didn't mean — I've been
right here. Working. You see?" He spoke mildly, as if to a
child who wakes up afraid in the dark, but also tensely, as if
the ogre in the closet waiting to attack might be real. "My
poor darling —"

"Don't patronize me." A silence. She slumped and stared.
Her voice became weak and drained of harmonics. "I'm
sorry I bothered you. Terribly sorry. I never will bother you
or anyone else again."

"Darling. Please. I'm so sorry about this — this. Let's
have our lunch now. I made a nice meal —" He put his hand
on her back. Was that a hump? Melpomene with a dowager's
hump? "You know you have to eat. You're the one who
asked me to help you with this. We've been all through this,
about the headaches, the rest —"

"I said, *Don't* you patronize me." She thrust him away
feebly, as if her arms had turned to water. Hiccoughing and
sobbing, she went on, the tendons of her neck rigid, her jaw
thrust out. "I hate you. You disgust me. You wrecked my

car. You're old. You're fat. You're lazy. You're stupid. You're pathetic in bed. I don't want you. I've never wanted you. I want a *man*. So don't you preach to me. I'm sick of your self-righteous babble."

Glorious to say these words, which she had only imagined in the past! Glorious to throw everything away. Glorious, having broken the cup, to break the plate! And see how his face collapsed and reddened; he was in pain! It was only fair; the judgment had fallen upon him; he deserved what he was getting. Why couldn't he take it like a man instead of like an old lady, dithering and doddering? Glorious to repay him after all the hurts she had suffered at his hands! The words could never be brought back inside her mouth. Panting, tears hot in the corners of her eyes, she enjoyed her victory.

A string of words clattered on the floor of his brain: I will never recover from this. His stomach convulsed; his blood rushed away. "But I waited for you — I had lunch ready for you. The lunch was especially for you. I waited and waited. You didn't say anything about postponing an appointment. You said you had to check your messages, and after that you said you had an emergency visitor. And you agreed —"

"You're saying *I* lied? Our marriage is over, then."

"What? I thought — you said we were going to have lunch together. And — and —" He was unable to go on thinking.

Look at him cringe! Everything was utterly clear now. An intolerable beast; not one more second of this. Her suitcase in the closet; cash, her escape money, in her desk; the bottles of pills turned over to her by suicidal people waited behind the New Jerusalem Bible in the bookcase. On the way to the plane, she would stop and purchase the dress. She would pass by Kuno's. The weather was turning bad. Wear the sable. James was so lazy he would never write his book and so there would never be awards banquets. A car door was slamming. That's right, Ellen Brent's appointment. He was fumbling, his eyes half-closed because he could not bear to witness the truth; from her he would receive only the truth. To harm her was to lose her forever. Now the bells below were jangling, and James was whining on and on. "Sh!" she said. "Someone is downstairs!"

"This is more important," he whispered. If they did not resolve the matter now, if she did not apologize —

With her face taut, deep grooves around her mouth, she bared her teeth. "You make me sick." Her voice was low and rasping. "*I* don't abandon people. I hope you die!"

What a marvelous day! Ellen toyed with the strip of leather sewn with bronze temple bells on the waiting-room door. She herself had given them to the Reverend.

The Reverend opened the study door. Her eyes were lustrous, her cheeks pink, as if she had just returned from an invigorating walk. If Ellen was not mistaken, the Reverend was trying to curb her delight, to adopt a more dignified pose while in fact she deeply shared Ellen's excitement, oh, about just being alive. If Ellen was not mistaken, she herself was the best, the smartest, and the most favored of all the fellowship. She headed the committee for the homeless; she was in charge of the after-service coffee hour; she organized the philosophy-group reading list. How dull church had been before the new Reverend's arrival! It had not even been a church; rather, it had been more like a car wash, everything done mechanically. Now, people were opening like beautiful flowers; yes, that was just how Ellen saw it. She would say that, at the right moment. And today the Reverend even wore a flowered skirt, and what elegant black pumps! And, on her little finger, a gold band.

"How wonderful you look," Ellen exclaimed. She handed the Reverend a bottle of sherry and, in a polished wooden box, two glasses of cut crystal. Slipping off her new jacket, she held it up for a moment in case the Reverend should want to admire the white fur trim.

"Very lovely, Ellen, dear. And what is this?"

"The sherry is imported, very special. I thought that now that winter's coming you might like to have an afternoon sip every once in a while."

They spoke about clothes for a few minutes, and then the Reverend took her chair and folded her hands and cleared her throat. The signal for them to enter the other realm.

"Well!" said Ellen, sitting down on the sofa. Because she never knew what the Reverend, in her straight-spined tranquillity, might speak about, and, besides, she understood Ellen. Ellen, on her first visit, had asked about some lines from St. Matthew: "The light of the body is the eye; if therefore thine eye be single, thy whole body shall be full of light: but if thine eye be evil, thy whole body shall be full of darkness. If therefore the light that is in thee be darkness, how great is that darkness!" The Reverend was immediately able to apply the scripture to Ellen's conduct even though they had just met. Her accuracy was astonishing. She wanted to help Ellen. The Reverend must have asked her a thousand questions — about her husband, her children, even her cat. From the Reverend, Ellen had begun to learn

how to refine herself, to enlarge her consciousness, to behave not in the ordinary way but as someone who hopes to
create a heaven on earth. The Reverend was unlike any
conventional minister; she was goodness personified; everyone knew that. Her intuition was magical. Without the
Reverend, Ellen would have eventually grown numb from
boredom. Now they were together, alone, about three feet
apart, but closer than Ellen ever was to anyone else. Even
though she cherished her husband and children, she couldn't
really talk to them. And with the Reverend, you could
discuss Spinoza or hemlines.

"I just have to tell you, I finished the *Philosophical Investigations* last night," Ellen said.

"The what?"

"You know, Wittgenstein."

"Oh." The Reverend pursed her lips. She seemed oddly
uninterested.

"Since you mentioned that you were reading it, I went out
and got a copy. What did you think of his remarks about
being held captive by a picture — of time as a stream, for
instance? And what about the idea that language creates
reality?"

" '*Wovon man nicht sprechen kann, darüber muss man schwei-
gen.*' Whereof one cannot speak, thereof must one be silent."

"Oh, right. The *Tractatus*. But I meant the ideas he de-
velops in the *Investigations*. I got so excited I couldn't sleep
last night. I'd love to put it on the list."

"I wouldn't do that, dear. People don't have time for that.
Entre nous, it's a bunch of nonsense."

"Really? You said — I thought —"

"I think you need to come down to earth and put your mind on your marriage, Ellen."

"But — everything is fine. At least it seems to be."

"You said you thought your husband was ignoring you. That he was too involved in his work —"

"I don't remember."

"Just after I arrived here, you said he was always working overtime, and then he was busy with your daughter's basketball games and so he couldn't come to the philosophy group."

"Well, he was helping coach last year. But now that's over, and I —"

"Why do you think what he did was so bad? He was being a good father. And he was trying to earn a little extra money. And you played the victim. You created an entire fantasy so you could justify feeling hurt. The truth is, I think you must ignore him quite often — you're always so busy with the fellowship."

"Oh," Ellen said. "But —"

"You have a habit of lying to yourself, my dear, dear Ellen," the Reverend said, "and that's always bad, because you know very well that you're lying."

"But I —"

"Please. Now you're lying to me. That's bad enough. But when you lie to yourself! It's useless. Absurd. Meaningless. Because you know that you're lying to yourself, so you aren't really lying to yourself. It's a completely sterile activity. Give it up, right this moment!"

Why was the Reverend suddenly so severe? Ellen blushed, and she began to cry.

"And you get used to believing your lies, even though

you know very well that you're lying. And you lie because you're afraid you can't bear the truth — even though you secretly know what it is. You're afraid of your own insignificance. Ellen, dear? Are you following? Oh, Ellen — don't be so upset. How many times have I told you not to be swayed by what others say? *I* don't think you're insignificant! I'm just trying to reveal something to you. I used a strong example so you'd really listen. We're having a little lesson in — in philosophy. In ethics. How can we find happiness in ourselves and right conduct with others? Give me some examples. Quick, now — we don't have more than a few minutes."

"Very lovely, Ellen, dear." Her voice, robust and kind, rose from below.

He strained to listen. They were discussing a jacket. The reproduction of *Woman Weighing Gold,* with its flat dull inks on paper, mocked him. He closed the book. What had he done wrong? As soon as she was alone, he would go down and apologize. But that might make her more violent. A voice in his head said: No matter what you do, she will cause monstrous trouble for you. And yet no one was sweeter or more loving. Ridiculous, her outbursts! Around the world, in wars and cataclysms and droughts, people were dying horribly, perhaps her own mother was at this very moment preparing to kill herself, and Melpomene was livid and angry about lunch. The voice said: Never again will you have any peace.

Mauritius painted one self-portrait. In *Canal Scene* his face could be read in the water, the sky, the spires, the serene row of buildings, one red-brick house a bit atilt, the glimpse down a passageway into a rear courtyard with a garden where three black-clad women conversed. James longed to leave himself behind and to cross the bridge over the canal and enter that town, quiet except for footsteps now and then on the cobbles or the sound of an oar pulling through water. If only he could step into that eternal summer afternoon! In the houses, next to windows with open shutters that let in swaths of clean light, under maps or paintings, women poured milk or kneaded bread or pierced fabric with needles or read letters or drew their fingers across the strings of a lute. A servant girl dozed, chin in hand, while a man looked on from another room. Next to a church with weeds growing between the stones sat a soldier smoking a long pipe. A couple leaned on a table and drank from big goblets; in the background, a doorway to an empty room with a mirror and a polished floor. Spaces opened onto other spaces; worlds were contained within worlds. When someone spoke, his voice was calm and honest.

James wasn't supposed to appear while Melpomene was seeing people, or even to walk on the stairs because his step would be heard in the study. The visitor might then ask who else was in the house, and how was Mr. Gilman (they all thought his name was Gilman), and then precious time would be wasted on small talk and nonsense — how long had they been married, how had they met — and she hated, she said, to talk about herself. "My overscruple," she called it. It was her work, and he had to respect it. Usually he even enjoyed practicing soft movements, like an Indian brave on the hunt, or a stealthy lover who must evade a jealous husband. But today he found himself imprisoned, desperate

to have Melpomene repair the destruction she had un-
leashed, to put her hand on his forehead and her lips on his.

He would do anything, anything to avert her rages. If only
he could find the reason for them, he would be able to prevent them. She had once agreed, after an explosion in his
presence that had been directed at Ruth when Melpomene
had found them laughing together, that perhaps it was a
matter of nutrition and rest. But she went on starving and
exhausting herself, and when he urged her to stop, she
screamed that he was not her mother. He sought other
causes. He tried, he really did, to make his behavior faultless,
and in her presence to be cautious. She would then cry, which
unnerved him, and accuse him of stiffness and wariness. And
the matter of the car. His car had been in the shop and he had
borrowed hers. The next day she found a dent in the fender.
She went white; she screamed. "You wrecked my car because you secretly want to hurt me. I know this. I know it
absolutely. I have direct knowledge; I understand your mind
better than you do." He swore to her that he would rather put
out his eyes with red-hot irons than cause her a second of
pain. In the end, he apologized, she gathered him into her
arms, and he felt he had atoned for his transgression.

If he closed his eyes, he could escape to a smaller, dimmer
house. But in that house lived dread.

Melpomene had calls to make as soon as Ellen left. Important calls. She must remember. Suddenly she was exhausted. A dark, flawed feeling passed over her. Beareth all
things, believeth all things, hopeth all things, endureth all
things.

Ellen was hesitantly saying something about her marriage, about how lucky she was. Sixteen years! (How thoroughly boring. What use could they possibly have anymore for each other?)

"Could God have brought this man to me?"

"Yes," Melpomene said, summoning up her powers. This was efficiency, a saving of fifteen or twenty minutes; if she did not make certain that Ellen left in a quiescent mood, a phone call would follow, and perhaps more questions about the *Philosophical Investigations,* when all Melpomene had read — and could scarcely recall except for the last line — were parts of the *Tractatus.*

The Reverend's smile and her yes were so exultant that Ellen was assured that her destiny had been arranged for all time. As she was leaving, she swept up her jacket, knocking to the floor a vase containing a dried bouquet of roses. When it broke, she wanted to weep again.

"It's all right," the Reverend murmured, kneeling and brushing the shattered flowers into her hand. "It means I really helped you today. We always have strange reactions to the person who helps us. Remind me to explain that to you. Or maybe I'll give a talk about it. And the vase cost me a dollar. I have another one in the garage just like it. And forget Wittgenstein. He's not for you, dear."

Seven

"DON'T YOU THINK you really should go to your mother?" he said. "I'm dying to see you, but —"

The bell at the Catholic church chimed three. Shame harrowed her: she had submitted to her stupid impulse to phone him a second time (mortifying enough that she had already left a message on his machine which she could not erase). All she had intended was to offer forgiveness. What followed was a magnetic disturbance rather than a conversation; her brain couldn't contain it; she saw her hand slamming down the receiver.

Afterward, breathing erratically, she enumerated the main points.

1. At first he was pleased; he seemed excited to hear from her. His voice was warm and loving. Ah, he wanted her.

2. Assured of his affection, she opened herself up to him. She told him her marriage was intolerable and begged — *begged!* — him to rescue her.

3. He heard the tremor in her voice. She hated him for that, and for the frozen modulation he adopted, as if he were speaking to an unreasonable pet. No, he did not want her.

Besides (she now dropped the inventory, which had failed to provide her with control of the matter), no one ought to be permitted to observe her unless she had assented; unless she had attained perfection (as she did on Sunday mornings). No one ought to see her wild in the ecstasy of lovemaking or crushed and uncontrollably sobbing.

Usually others, wallowing in their own pigpens, perceived nothing; no one called her on her slips. Ellen would never have any inkling that Melpomene had been unable to bring herself to read the *Philosophical Investigations;* the foolish woman had been completely confounded by the German and the sudden change in topic. Each day Melpomene could close the door behind her, sigh, and congratulate herself on once again turning in an excellent performance. Once again she had escaped judgment. But if by chance someone did notice, if by chance James insisted on his version of events — as he so tiresomely had lately — and even produced some sort of proof, then she would be forced to work hard (more work, and already she was extraordinarily weary) to erase those notions, because if he maintained them he couldn't possibly love her. She herself would certainly not be able to love anyone who deceived her.

But suppose God — there must be a God because Kuno had been given the seat next to her on the plane (the turbulence had frightened her; he had soothed her with the explanation that if the rolls in the fluid motion could be counted and the resulting pattern of numbers made into an image, she would see the beautiful geometry that shaped everything, from the milk spreading through their jiggling coffee to the formation of storm clouds outside the plane window to the miniature mountain range of ice crystals on the window itself) — suppose God could see her imperfections? Ever since childhood the force of this surmise never failed to overwhelm her.

People had to understand that she couldn't approach others (unless they were members of her fellowship, of course, or other wretches in extremis); they had to allow for her shame, her shyness, her utter terror of being refused. Kuno, hearing her quaver, ought to have been solicitous. He ought to have understood her suffering, as she had always so exquisitely monitored his. He chose to suffer — chose it! — instead of decisively choosing to be with her. She'd mentioned Mother only to show what torments fate was delivering these days. But Kuno had seized on the sorrow and twisted it against her. "You really should go to your mother." My God, how dare he? What was said next? She had no idea; her mouth moved, her heart beat; her righteous wrath thrust itself forth. Air flowed out of her mouth, impelled by contractions of her vocal chords; the vibrations entered Kuno's ear as words of some sort, and satisfied — no, intoxicated — with a job well done, she had banged down the receiver.

The bells at the Methodist church rang three. (So much for ecumenicism.) She would work, that was all. Whatsoever thy hand findeth to do, do it with all your might, for there is no work, nor device, nor knowledge, nor wisdom, in the grave whither thou goest. She paced and began taking books from shelves and opening them to passages she might use. People were poorly read and didn't recognize borrowings. The topic would either be the Futility of Self-Deception or Our Eternity or The Meaning of the Garden. She turned to Genesis. Was that a car in the drive? No, she really couldn't see anyone right now. . . . Had she just destroyed all hope?

Oh, God. Why had she reacted like that? All she wanted was to be pure and harmonious. (The rows of happy upturned faces on a Sunday morning; the fragrance of aftershave and perfume and freshly oiled woodwork; the rustling of good clothes.) She would cancel the rest of the day's appointments, forget the lecture, and go far away, to a place where her nastiness would not bother anyone; she would take nothing. She could make herself very small, completely unobtrusive. At least she possessed the sensitivity never to intrude. That was one of her best traits: she never bothered a soul.

They would have to beg her to return. And of course she would forgive, because she believed in love above all, and absolution. She would forgive Kuno. Drive to the city and ring his bell. Yes. She would stand there mute, shy, generous, wearing the dress. He was used to seeing her in dark colors; he would be taken aback. And the gold band. . . . Her skin tingled and tears welled up, bending the room. Had the event already happened? For an instant it seemed so. Didn't she go to him and humbly gaze up at him, her mouth half open, and hadn't the dam of his ambivalence at last broken? And all his love came rushing toward her! What a triumph! (Although he would be rendered helpless, she would still reserve a safe place for herself, an uncommitted corner.)

First she would have to describe what the garden was, is.

What could it be, in one's life? "And they were both naked, the man and his wife, and were not ashamed." She hadn't yet lost the game; at least he had not seen her fall to the floor and writhe and scream and then curl up in a ball and sob. He had taken her near the boundary of what she knew as herself, or perhaps past it. A conspiracy: with him, her body followed its own wishes while she helplessly watched. And after dominating her completely, he would leave. He had to lock himself up in his studio and paint, he had to get some sleep, he was expected at the museum ball, he had to fly to an opening in Chicago. Sometimes she won by leaving first, but in the end it came to the same perfidy. And had she succeeded in wounding him, even a little, by choosing James?

She made notes. "And they heard the voice of the Lord God walking in the garden in the cool of the day: and Adam and his wife hid themselves. . . ." The time had been brief in paradise; Eve had destroyed everything, or the serpent had, or Adam, in allowing Eve to do what she wanted, or perhaps God had. The punishment for eating the fruit had been death, but then God amended it; He cast them out, telling the woman, "I will greatly multiply thy sorrow. . . ." And the man: "Dust thou art, and unto dust shalt thou return." What aggression! The poor man scarcely understood his misdeed or its consequences. The human race had lost paradise; it had received the knowledge of good and evil and also the experience of death. She was struck anew by the old seminary debate: How unjust God was! But no — we always want to go toward heaven, and we're always dragged down to the earth. Well, that was an evasion, that was blaming God, blaming the machinery. Really we don't want paradise. An example here of how people inevitably embrace what destroys them while ignoring what sustains them. Unfair, then — it must be an impersonal flaw, in the substance of being. Souls yearn to rise and bodies to fall. . . . In the garden, we did not know the meaning of mortality or consciousness. (Ah, we still don't know!) We were impatient, and we were thrown out. Too impatient, too lazy to regain paradise. Between us and paradise, cherubim and a flaming sword which turned every way to guard the tree of life. Unto dust shalt thou return. And Kuno had had the arrogance to tell her to go see her own mother!

In the garage she would find a stool and a rope. The dim, mildewy cavern was crammed with things: a broken vacuum cleaner, bicycles with flat tires, chairs to be recaned so that they could replace the horrors in the dining room, dozens of cartons. From a box of glassware, she pulled out a vase etched with laurel leaves. She owned perhaps ten sets of dishes and six sets of flatware, all bought at auctions. She was afraid of death. All of the time.

The telephone rang. Vase in hand, she ran back to the house and grabbed the instrument as if it were alive and about to escape. But it was only Edgar, who said he had a migraine and so he and Raymond wouldn't be able to come for counseling today.

Melpomene hid her fury and told him she hoped he felt better soon and advised him to have something to eat and to lie down with a cold compress over his eyes. The couple was always about to break up; if it weren't for Melpomene, they would have long ago. Raymond was continually manufacturing trouble for Edgar, who was very charming, and earnest in his struggle to stop using drugs. Raymond refused to believe him when he told the truth. It was only when Raymond persuaded Edgar to lie, to accept all the blame, that Raymond was content, hollowly content. Each of them privately hoped he would find a better partner, an ideal one, in fact. Melpomene, who peered down upon their lives and could see the entire landscape, tried to show the men that they had a strong bond; they both said that their years together had been happy. She tried to teach them that there were no ideal partners. To tolerate and serve each other. Only in that way would Edgar feel secure enough to stop his addiction. And for a few days, Raymond would remember, but by the next week Edgar was calling again.

God, how hard she worked, how many thousands of hours she had spent with the miserable, the impoverished, the sick, the dying!

A whole hour free. Terrible, like an hour of insomnia in the middle of the night. No time to schedule anything. Not enough time to drive to town to buy the dress, and why do that when Kuno had told her she ought to stay with her mother? She might as well get some low-heeled shoes out of the poor box and tie a scarf under her chin and spend all her free time in intensive care waiting rooms with other washed-up, middle-aged children.

The branches of the willow stroked the roof shingles; the refrigerator hummed; a whole hour, empty. She would not go back to the garage. She would not search out the stool and the rope. She would not run water in the bathtub and get in it with James's razor.

She was in control. Once at a world religion conference in San Francisco, she had shown a lama the Golden Gate

Bridge and told him that people jumped from it. Why? he exclaimed. To kill themselves, she replied. Why? he asked. She explained. But they'll be reborn in exactly the same circumstances, he said, surprised.

She needed to face her life squarely and correct her sins. To beat down these horrid, alien impulses. But wasn't that being rigid? No, she had to clean up her mess before the day ended. She dialed Kuno's number and hung up when his machine answered. Later, when she could govern her voice. She called her mother, and the maid said she was napping. Quietly she went upstairs to promise James that she would never behave like that again. I don't know what came over me; I don't know why I said that. Can you forgive me? I forgive you for what you did in bed this morning. All better? Let's go for a walk. In his study, the computer whirred, but he was absent. As she passed the bedroom door, the mirror altered its picture: she became a pale ripple in the shadowy room. He was nowhere to be found, thank God.

Free, she would turn her back and simply walk away, walk until she dropped. She went outside and along the drive that led through the woods. She would go and go. Fly to Paris and live in some horrible little room. Or find a monastic retreat in the English countryside. If it weren't for Kuno's punishing curtness, she could have spent the hour talking to him, arranging their meeting at that inn in the forest to the north. Now an hour was going to be wasted. It didn't contain enough time for her to concentrate on her lecture. No, she would walk. She would lose weight. She would walk every day — five, ten miles. Perhaps she would organize a walking group. She would stride at the head of a band of smiling hikers. Perhaps an attractive and brilliant man, new in town, would join in.

Men are not like us, she told herself. They lack the necessary emptiness inside, an emptiness that resonates with the great emptiness that encloses the world. They are arranged on green fields; they move in ranks. Their hearts beat differently. They come from us and forget us and return to us, like dreamers awakening from a dream. After a third of a mile, out of breath, she stopped at the abandoned cemetery.

The forest had grown right up to the rail fence. The tombstones, flaking, effaced, some altogether blank, tilted this way and that in the bent grass, which was littered with puckered, vinegary apples that had dropped from a gnarled tree.

She stretched out on her back. Her clothes would get stained, but what did it matter? Who cared what she looked like? One day she would be dead. Alone on a catafalque under a single harsh light, and then in a hole in the ground. Those who had claimed to love her might weep, finally, but she would be dead, dead, dead. She would continue to *be*, of course. That was the horror. Her body would go right on with its messy bacterial business, a lump of dead, decaying meat. The flesh would go. Her hand would become nothing but converging rows of metacarpal bones, her skull a hollow shell, barren of thought and memory. Eventually not one living person would know her name. If memory clung to mineral, the bones would remember. And what would they remember? Betrayals: Kuno standing in front of the café kissing that woman; Kuno in the parking lot telling Melpomene goodbye forever. He, too, would be nothing but a skull one day. And so would all the others. The skulls might contain memory traces of her — who knew? And when the sun expanded, the oceans boiled away, and rivers of red, molten rock consumed the cemeteries of the world, the skulls, which had each enclosed a universe, would burst into flame, would be refined into some harder element or jewel, and yet a trace might remain — of an embrace, of this autumn day, of a hand reaching for a maroon washcloth, of an eye looking at itself.

The clouds, their undersides ashen, passed in silence: they did not exist. The crown of the ancient apple tree stirred: it did not exist. The grass, vividly green, scattered with withered leaves, the strutting crow with its cold, insolent eye and shiny wings, the slivering fence posts, the tombstones: they did not exist. They were only patterns formed by explosions at the tips of neuronal twigs inside her skull. And inside the skulls of others, she was nothing, a mere chemical event, a constellation of neurons firing. She did not exist.

But she could not believe that. She wanted to be immortal. If there were an elect, if God had chosen her, then she was immortal and did not have to worry. But if there were no elect, then she was the same as anyone else — as Kristen (she had to remember to call the psychiatrist), or Suzanne (ah, God, the spot on her lung; suppose Melpomene had that; it was possible; she was always worn out, too, and hadn't had a checkup in years), or Ellen, or James, or the cleaning woman, or the people who lived in the bus terminal.

But she wasn't the same; that was obvious; anyone could see that. She shone; they were only shadows. She had perceived her own soft shining when she was twenty and had sat in Notre-Dame, which was shaped like a body, the body of the archaic mother goddess, ribbed and vaulted, and from the dim interior, dappled with blurred patterns of colored light, resounded a deep pulse, and she had gazed up at the center of the rose window and understood everything without understanding anything. The way to immortality had to be through self-perfection, as conscious as light passing through stained glass. She swore then that each day she would do something to burnish herself. If she succeeded, then she would survive the others, survive her bones, the fire, the infinite emptiness.

If only she could live with Kuno (she clutched a handful of grass), she would achieve the calm needed to lead a conscious life rather than a mechanical one. But first she had to convince him that his very salvation lay in her power. Didn't he know? His letter had awakened her: she was in hell. But of course he was no solution. She let go of the grass.

Why did this revelation make her so still? Because, she supposed, it gave her a rest from striving. She needed only to be like the sky, the wind, the tree. Yes, she must apologize to both hapless men; her terrible words to them had become hooked into the permanent fabric of the world and might somehow resonate forever, the way light continues traveling out and out from a star that exploded millions of years ago; the least she could do would be to send some decent words outward to nullify the bad ones. Both men, and all the others, poor babies, had trusted her and she had exploited them, and then given up on them when she tired of them. Not a very lovely portrait. But a true one. The skull the repentant Magdalene contemplates is her own. *You must change your life.*

But hadn't men led Magdalene down that path? Was she entirely to blame? Had she asked for the body of a woman, with all its mad desires? Melpomene had certainly not requested this earth, with its oppressively blue sky and agitated clouds and cold bed of damp grass. Nevertheless, she had tried to do her best. (Batter my heart, three-personed God!) James, her cross: intrusive and stingy and deceitful, even petty, claiming to want to have lunch with her and then dumping her. And when he did apologize, when he did give her some gift or other, creeping up to her, head down, the guilt coursing from his face like a poisonous sweat, she despised him. Spineless. No, she had to win everything for herself. Except once. She and Kuno had stood naked before the mirror, and he had slipped the ring onto her little finger. Forever, she had said. If she were to die today, right now, lying here utterly alone in the cemetery, they would find the ring on her finger. She could use the pills. She had to remember to add a codicil to her will demanding that she be buried with the ring.

In death she would rest.

Her watch said 4:18. The bones around her eyes ached. She had taken a chill. There was nowhere to go but back to the house.

The interior was black; she had to blink; her cheeks were cold. The rooms lightened to gray, and the webs in her vision dissolved. In the corner of her office, a low, angled ray of sun caught a ball of dust. Her fingernails were dirty and broken. She stroked her throat — did she really have wattles now, like her mother? *After I'm gone,* her mother was always saying, had been saying for decades. Melpomene had tried to transform her mother and had failed. A few months ago she had called Melpomene and said, "After I'm gone, I don't want all my money going for taxes. I'm setting up a trust so that you have the use of it right now." But then she forgot. Just forgot. She would die, and the estate would be gutted. Melpomene only existed when her mother happened to think of her; she imagined Melpomene always to be at her disposal. She concocted melodramas; she threw tantrums, working herself up into theatrical sobs. Now she was living on merely out of spite, and threatening to kill herself out of hatred. Melpomene had phoned her, though; the maid was the witness.

Eight

ON THE PATH along the edge of the field, near some small, dense cedars, he bent over and examined a tuft of gray, all that remained of the hawk's prey. One instant it had been a mockingbird or a catbird in flight; the next, a ball of feathers floating down, flesh, beak, and claws consumed.

Once he had occupied the body of a child, a moving, transparent sphere, whole, aware, wordless. He couldn't recall that, really. Only the idea of it. He couldn't even recall what it was he had understood so simply and so well when he had awakened today. The bathing girl, gazing over her shoulder, lips slightly, sensuously, parted to show tongue and teeth; the forest, the tangled brown forest and blue uplands; Melpomene whispering to him. But what was behind all that? This morning, as he watched the two swans rise and take wing, it had seemed easy for him to lean his head against the sky and beat his way forward. But his wife had bruised her thigh. His wife had spoken to someone on the phone. His wife had opened her mouth and screamed at him.

In the wrack line he found a dead fish, a dead gull, an old shoe. The sky was pulling apart from the land, letting go except for a long, brassy finger here and there. Wherever his eye fell, disorder was revealed. The balance of the picture had been distorted from the beginning, as in *The Wedding of Burgher van Dam,* in which Mauritius had deliberately placed the bedposts, with their gargoyle finials, in the wrong plane so that the sneering beasts appeared to taunt the union. He even painted a flawless rosary of crystal beads, each one containing a perfect glassy, global reflection, hanging from a finial to call attention to the deformation.

In the most gracious of landscapes, death had always predominated, but James had never cared to see the relent-less attention nature has for murder. He had entered into an unconscious collaboration with its foul deeds, thinking himself a beloved child for whom exceptions would be made. Well, an ordinary thought; but he was a man of limited perceptions, was he not? No one escaped from the absurd fact of the commonplace. Here he was tethered, powerless, worthless. (*Old, fat, disgusting.*) She did not love him. He gripped the shell in his pocket as if that would stop his fall.

He would simply speak to her in a rational way. My mistake — our mistake. Mistake? (*Pathetic in bed.*) Maybe you always do exactly what you like. No — that would infuriate her. Everything depended on this marriage; he would not be able to go on without it. Best to keep it simple: the universe is a stark, cold place. (She would approve of that observation.) I love you. I never meant to hurt you. I was hungry and I ate. That's all.

As soon as her last visitor had left, he would quell his fear and take her hand. They would walk along the beach. He would show her all the killing, the withered stalks. He would ask her if she thought they were somehow going to be exempt from the erosion of nature. He would say it outright, clearly and in a kindly tone. He would give examples. She would have to acknowledge her wrong behavior and make amends.

He had never before tried to weave together what he had observed about her. Dozens of instances now came to mind. In an argument, she would try anything, and while he stood before her, numb and stammering and struggling to recall what he meant to say, she was swiftly setting traps, using distractions, evasions, and lies: all because she had to win. And if she thought she were losing, she either left or became pale and trembling and tearful. In either case, he was destroyed.

He stopped. Wrong of him to think of her so cynically. Better to overlook the whole matter. That's what he had done in the past. She usually forgot whatever was disturbing her and, soon, assisted by his apologies, her former affection returned. She would give him an expensive art book or a silk tie and come up behind him and massage his neck, and his gratitude would overwhelm his doubts. But how could he erase what she had said today? (*Never wanted you.*) Suppose he could just talk to her. He would say, You must not treat me in this way. You hurt me. Besides, I need my freedom. I might want to go somewhere and just spend some time by myself. You won't even notice I'm gone. Or, he might say, You'd like to go someplace yourself, on your own. Oh, no — she might whisper on the phone. (*Dearest . . . meet . . . still love. . . .*)

He went ten paces. The speech would show that he meant no harm. But she might hiss at him and shove him away, and threaten to kill herself. She might lock herself upstairs with the razors (had he remembered to hide them? He had). And then he would have to wait, nauseated with terror, calling through the door to her, listening to her movements, a hundred maneuvers going through his head. That was how it had happened the last time, after she had found the dent in the fender. Or suppose she listened to him impassively and then ran down into the bay? What had happened to her other men (until now he had always thought of them as oafish and mean) when she brandished her own death at them?

A bank of drab cloud thickened over the water. A chill wind sprang up. Miles of shells, stones, quills, spines, were tossed up on the beach by the muttering thrust of the waves. A bird cried overhead in the yellowing dome of the sky. The leaves of the shrubs were leathery and faded. The ticking shadows of the stalks, weaker now, continued to move, thin and long. His palms were creased with dirt. He had washed his hands just a short while ago, but now they were filthy.

Freedom, he would say. Anything to have his life back, unused, lustrous, rising up full of promise! Freedom is the most — Bark flaked from the bare trunks, leaving pale hieroglyphics. Birds fled. The golden hoops of grass in the field went dull. He would go home, to his house, the house that his great-grandfather had built on the land an ancestor had bought from an Indian chieftain. He would make everything clean and new again.

"I'd been on the road for years. Brain was starting to fail. Couldn't remember the words to my own songs. Everyone always asked me to do 'Mallarmé's Dream,' and I couldn't think of a single line. And the riffs. The riffs I had composed! Too hard for me. My best guitar disappeared at the end of the last show when we were mobbed on stage, and I didn't even care."

The Reverend nodded encouragingly.

"What I'm saying, it's confidential. You won't tell anyone?"

"Never! Absolutely not!"

"Kristen said I could count on you." Gabriel Porter had not wanted an appointment with this lady minister. But Kristen, whom he had loved more than anyone in his life before or since their affair, and whom he was now thinking of taking up with again if she could pull herself together, had told him that the Reverend Gilman was better than any guru or astrologer, and that if it weren't for her, Kristen would not be alive. Gabriel was not sure whether he himself was alive. And this Reverend struck him as humorless and bourgeois, judging from her knickknacks. Probably once attractive, in a housewifely way; when she took her chair, she had slid her skirt up to her knees. And it was quite pleasurable to receive her unwavering scrutiny.

"Go on," she said softly. In the first hour she would learn everything she needed to know about this man, and by the second hour, simply by accepting all that he said, by floating along with him, she would have him half in love with her, and then she would show him the truth about himself. Ever since childhood, when she knew with excruciating accuracy what her mother and father were feeling, she could sense exactly the sorrow and discord within the person across from her; she became that person; but a part of her remained separate, observing, thinking of how to help. The evangelicals called it a gift of the Holy Spirit, the gift of discernment. But they had a ceiling on their intellects, and she did not, and so she believed it must come from her own profound love of others. She couldn't turn it off, either; it happened to her with Kuno, with James, with whomever. . . . Before Gabriel came, she had put what remained of the dried roses in the new vase, and brushed her hair, and sprayed on perfume. If he could be led to a deep, healing understanding, then he might mention his gratitude to Melpomene in a magazine interview, and Kuno might read it and regret having ever hurt her. Oh, what a beast she was. She knew that. Worse than anyone she knew, worse than the worst louse-ridden, smelly bus-terminal resident. Worse than this trembling man with his graying curls, his earring, and a ring on every finger. One of the jewels, a big diamond, pained her eyes, and she had to control her gaze to prevent her headache from getting stronger. Her punishment. If she had been good, by now she would surely have been rewarded. Let the glittering people pursue their frivolous pastimes; she would go to the garage, find a rope. Her lusts and rancor had ridden her for long enough.

"The drummer had given me something for the flight home, and I'd take a step or say a word and feel and hear myself a fraction of a second later. Know what I mean? Had to make up a kind of plot about what was going on: I'm in this movie, I'm going home all messed up, and so I have to act in this certain way, see? There was a heavy fog and I could barely drive. When I woke up, it was daytime. This dark woman in white was there, with this girl wearing shorts and sunglasses, kind of flirty." He smiled to himself

and for an instant his bravado faded, and he became endear-
ingly cherubic and sad. No wonder Kristen wanted to take
care of him. "I watched them opening and closing their
mouths. Then I got it. I was on the deck of my own house.
Woman was the maid. Girl was my daughter. I said, 'How
did you get so big?' You follow?"

Melpomene let her eyes widen slightly. "Yes. I understand." She had never worn white because it was for maids
and nurses; better not to buy the dress. Suppose Kuno
apologized. That would push her over the very edge. The
fall would begin. He didn't understand. He seldom let her
get her way, but when he did, she hated him even more. If he
happened to be brusque, she hated him (at the same time
desiring him in the most grueling extreme) because he
showed what she had known all along — that he lacked even
the most rudimentary interest in her, in knowing her, in
rescuing her. In any case, Gabriel would be grateful to her.
Hadn't Kristen said he was a great lover? And wasn't
Melpomene being an elitist, a snob, to dismiss his kind of
music? Anyway, he knew Mallarmé — that was something.
She'd have to find a book of his in James's library and copy
out a poem for Gabriel. And wasn't his music the real
culture of the present — of the future? And perhaps he knew
important people; she would travel on private jets, buy new
clothes, meet new, fascinating, powerful men. . . .

"Anyway, she giggles, and she doesn't want me to pick
her up, but I carry her around on the deck, and then I saw the
thing." He put his hands over his face, and his rings glinted.
"Uhh."

"You saw the 'thing'?"

"This wound. On her thigh. It was the shape of a spider,
and the blood had turned black."

The bruise James had caused Melpomene this morning; she could still feel the pang. "Oh, dear!"

"I said, 'Jesus Christ! What's that?' And she says, 'Nothing, nothing, forget it.' Says, 'I haven't been to sleep yet. I've got a million things to do,' and she leaves."

"How did you feel about that?" Why wouldn't he look at her? He kept addressing himself as if to an invisible being next to her. The sculpture — he was riveted by the angel. She could use that somehow.

"Well, I just went around opening doors. I hadn't been there in years, and my wife never managed to fix the place up before she left. The rooms have twenty-five-foot ceilings, and this was bothering me a lot —"

"You're in the Wyatt mansion, aren't you?" If she could ever persuade James to sell this ramshackle house, that place, oceanfront, would be a good investment. Perhaps Gabriel needed the money. Or, if she and he became lovers. . . .

"Yeah, I guess. All that air hanging up there. In the girl's room, there was lots of denim stuff — skirts, maybe twenty jackets. All new. And closets with stacks of baby clothes and baskets of toys."

Melpomene stretched out her legs and crossed them at the ankle. Her legs, at least, were still good. Since he was so interested in details, since he was such a great lover, let him get absorbed in her legs, let him see her nice feet in their custom-made pumps. "I'm with you, I hear you," she murmured.

He continued talking to the angel. "In the living room, the curtains were closed, so it was like it was under water. All kinds of games, pool table, Ping-Pong, slot machines, electronics, a gigantic jigsaw puzzle, a few things I couldn't figure out — a table with smooth stones and some pieces of rope."

"Rope?" The dark, flawed feeling came over her again.

"Oh, and a pennant that said Bardo State. And there were these plants around, too, and a huge aquarium with tropical fish."

Tires crunched on gravel. Perhaps it was Kuno, coming to apologize, so impassioned that he'd forgotten about James, and he would see Gabriel's red Maserati, and she would go to the door and say, Oh, she was busy. . . .

There was a knock, and the brass bells jingled. She smiled and sighed. "Please excuse me." As she passed the mirror she lifted her chin. She would be icy, very icy.

A policeman carrying a bag. James's body had been found — that was it. His effects. Oh, no. She would be alone now, in danger, and she would wear a black veil and walk bravely behind the coffin, and it was James, James, the only man who had ever truly loved her —

"Reverend Gilman?"

She was barely able to speak. "Yes, what is it?" She shielded her eyes from the sun.

The man, smooth as an egg, seemed a little embarrassed. "Congratulations, Reverend. You won the Police Athletic League raffle."

"Oh, how wonderful!" James, wherever he was, was probably still alive! Thank God. Let me remember this: let me remember that I love James, that it would kill me if anything bad happened to him. "A flashlight — I need this!"

"It's a high-power rechargeable flashlight, ma'am."

"Oh. Well. I'm really honored. Thank you." How striking he was! So young, so strong. Rosy with health, shyly grinning.

He pointed to the Maserati. "That looks like Gabriel Porter's."

With a little seductive laugh, she winked and memorized the name on his badge, Finley, in case she ever got a traffic ticket. "I'm a minister, you know. Confidentiality and all that. Now, if you can drop by later, I'll give you a cup of coffee for your trouble. How's that?"

Gabriel examined the mementos. Why all the pictures of herself? She wasn't a star, for Christ's sake. Maybe it cheered her up to see herself when she still had her looks, leaning against a Greek column with some old guy. Or were you supposed to be impressed? A letter of commendation from the war-criminal President — fantastic. Gabriel felt bleak. She was probably going to treat him the way everyone else except Kristen did.

Melpomene made her lips into a half kiss and emitted another little laugh and put the paper bag on the floor under the writing table. Was she too old to make Gabriel fall in love with her? Of course she didn't want him, but what would Kuno think when he learned? Suppose he turned on the car radio and heard a song called "Melpomene." Naturally, care would have to be taken with Kristen.

"I'm very sorry," she said. "It was the police. But everything is all right. Thank heavens. So often when they come it's bad news, and I have to blaze off to the hospital. Please, let's go on."

Gabriel flicked the nose of the angel and then sat down. "Well, there are other rooms I didn't even mention. All jammed full of stuff. Stuff I'd forgotten, or my wife had bought, that I'd never even wanted. Now I know where all my money went."

"So you're broke?"

"I still get royalties, but I'll never be rich again like that." The rueful cherub reappeared. "But I don't need much.

Anyway, the girl is out on one of the decks. And I'm, 'What's with all the rooms? Maybe you should use some of this stuff—learn scuba diving.' She pretends she's counting. Says, 'Dad, I am *talking* on the phone. *Please.*' She must have learned how to behave by watching kids on TV. I say, 'You don't do drugs, do you? I hope to God not. Shouldn't you get some sleep?' But she just ignored me."

"Ignored you? That must make you feel bad." He would come to rely on Melpomene.

"Yeah. So I went into my old bedroom and lay down. I thought about the maid taking care of the girl, watering the plants, feeding the fish, year after year. How many years? I can't keep fixed on what a year is. Sometimes when I close my eyes I see colored lights moving, and I'll hear a string being plucked and tuned, and I think that there are crowds around the bed, and I jump right up. That's those years. Well, today Kristen was telling me all these ideas of hers, and she may be on to something. She really thinks about these things. But anyway, I can't keep focused on what a year is, or a lot of years."

"Bergson, the philosopher —"

"How is a minute that passed ten years ago any different from a year that passed ten years ago? Think about it —"

"Bergson says —"

"So I figured that if I just lay there for a few hours I'd get straight, and the things would go away, all the stuff, her wound, the air up there. I'm still waiting. My thoughts and my body are still out of sync. I was always completely happy, completely inside the music. Now I'm spooked. Everything I wanted has gone up in smoke. I can't even remember what I wanted."

"You can't remember what you wanted. Maybe we can find a solution. Just remember that you know how to walk and talk and play an instrument, and those were very hard things to learn. You're capable of a lot." She heard a click, and the light on the answering machine began to blink. "We need to find out what's spooking you, and I'm sure we can." She lowered her voice and regarded him earnestly. "Meanwhile, you can begin to find a part of yourself that's calm. Like the angel here. You can make yourself very quiet and think of a time when you've been in the music — perfectly balanced and serene. You know, that moment is continuing in you now, somewhere, because we never lose anything, and I think it's going to come to the surface. Maybe not this instant, but soon. . . . I have an impression of you as immensely talented and forceful, but right now you're in flux. You're searching — that can be a fruitful, exciting time. I'd be very happy to help you. We've made a beginning today, and I'm sure that there's much more for us to discover. Would you like to see me again this week? I'm free almost any day except Sunday. And you're very welcome to come to the service, and afterward we have the philosophy-group luncheon." She wanted to say, You need me; I can take your hand, I can heal you. I've done it for others. He was getting up and he was reaching for the door. "Wait," she said. "Perhaps there's a book I can loan you, something that will help you until we get together again." She went to the shelves.

He shook his head. Too eager. She probably would call up some newspaper the minute he left: Gabriel Porter Turns to God. "That's OK. I'll — I'll have to get back to you. Thanks a lot. Really. Say, that's some sculpture."

"It's a copy of a Michelangelo. Well, a copy of an imitation of a Michelangelo."

"Looks like Kristen, a little. Except for the nose."

"I suppose it does. Dear Kristen, sweet little Kristen." Melpomene clenched her fist, driving her nails into her palm to remind herself to make the call. "Poor darling. My lamb."

"She says you've really helped her."

"I must tell you, she really tries. Would you like to have this?"

"The angel?"

"Please — take it, it's yours! To remind you of —"

"That's very nice of you, but I guess not. I mean, I have all that stuff already. Well, thanks. Bye."

He hadn't thought she was good enough. She knew the type: insecure, self-absorbed, preening. Beyond help.

Once again alone, the expression of professional goodwill slowly departing from her face, she saw James at the edge of the lawn, reduced, a tiny male insect that clings to the large body of the female. The Maserati roared away. She had been thrust into the frozen void yet again. The crowds, pretending to admire her, advanced toward her through the years with grotesque faces, ready to suck her blood. She would make them all disappear.

Nine

TODAY, TODAY. The mirror caught her in the low-slanting light. The thing she could not imagine happening to her had happened. (Easy to imagine lying under the grass for eons until the rivers of fire overflowed; hard to imagine this, today, while she still had eyes to see.) The thing had puckered the skin above her lip and creased her forehead; it had laid a web of fine lines over her cheeks and pleated her neck; it had humped her back and pushed out her stomach; it had made her legs spindly and knot-veined. Gradually, she had stopped noting the creases around her mouth, the hollows under her eyes; she had succeeded in seeing less and less of herself until she couldn't remember whether she had glanced in the mirror or not; or she would focus only on whether her hair was in place; or she would admire her lips in the shape of a kiss and think of a man closing his eyes in ecstasy. But she wouldn't look at herself head on. And so here, today, in the glare, the startling face of her mother appeared. "Ah," she murmured, the humiliation of it! Why didn't she just stop complaining and go ahead and kill herself? And why do *I* bother to go on living?

The telephone rang again. She turned on the volume of the answering machine and slowly stacked the books on her desk, lining up the spines. The Bible remained open to Genesis. Would she write a final talk? What Is Our Eternity? That would be fitting. It could be read as the eulogy. The upturned white faces, row after row in black, the coffin on the catafalque. . . . Or, What Has Become of the Garden? A rib was taken from Adam to make Eve, and they were happy together in the garden, ignorant of good and evil, and out of curiosity and the wish to be divine, Eve had betrayed him, and so the myth — very unfair, it was — could be seen as one of self-betrayal. But, of course, women, driven to know, to control, cursed to bring forth their children in pain and suffering, were always plotting betrayals; she saw that among the members of the fellowship. Scheming, small-minded, spiteful. Women got what they wanted and then were dissatisfied. The men: hopeless, weak, flabby. And limp. Not one of them could survive hearing the truth about himself. But it was God's fault in the first place, because —

The machine answered the call. Kuno. "I phoned a while ago and left a message. I hope you got it. Mel, you can't hang up on me like that. I want to know if everything is all right. Mel? Are you there?"

Wonderful. She observed herself. She was not crazy because she could observe herself. "Mel? Please pick up the phone if you hear me." How stupid and hypocritical of him. Of course everything was not all right. Let him squirm. She was not his slave. Her foot struck the paper bag under her desk. Whatever was she going to do with another flashlight?

"I'll try you again a little later."

She watched the machine blinking. She was in sublime control. Happy, in fact, surgingly, resplendently happy.

Up the stairs she went, a headless lump of shadow, the bannister, the paneling, the steps rising and falling around her. Never mind the disintegration of the body. All she had ever truly wanted was to become a saint. When she concentrated, when she made herself objective, when she was desperately needed, she achieved complete serenity and nothing disturbed her. When Edith Simon killed herself, hadn't Melpomene kept a vigil with Philip Simon in the room where the body lay? Her performance had been impeccable; she could see respect, even awe, in the eyes of the police when they arrived. She had been suffused with a divine force. Unperturbed, correct, she glided along; each step blended with the next; her gestures and words were exact; the world might be clouded, bloody, but she was clear. If only this instant she might be summoned to the emergency room, she would be saved.

This moment, right here, the little cranky window in the stairwell, the smell of earth, the rippled pane giving out onto lawn, tree trunks metallic, a brown tangle of leafless shrubbery, a pinkish stretch of beach, the cobalt water sprinkled with gold: all this ought to be enough. Enough for any given human being. Gratitude swelled her heart. She alone was sighted. She might love, she might hate. But she gazed steadily through transparent lenses at herself and the world. Two circles merged. She acknowledged her sins and affirmed that from this day on she would never repeat them. Tonight she would take James by the hand, and she would declare this so that he would be a witness to her sacred oath.

And she would call Kuno and also swear to him, and inform him with all the kindness she could gather that she was the friend of his soul but that their affair had ended. She would give up her romantic fantasies and hysteria and deception and malice. She would strive to be pure until the day came when she was as unhypocritically and effortlessly perfect, as intuitively perfect alone, as she was in public. She would grow in wisdom and beauty. Her watch said 6:06. All she had to do was what she taught others: to find that eternal moment of tranquillity and rest within it. Hadn't she shown that to James, dear James?

She knew James. Oh, she knew him. His every move and thought. Hidden in his study, in the back of a desk drawer — that was where he must keep the gun.

She gazed through the warped pane in the stairwell. A bird swam past. An immense shadow moved across the lawn. She had been dumped like a sack of garbage, forced to stay in a body that was wrinkling, thickening, stiffening, bowing.

James, his eyes down, slowly started toward the house, veered away, stopped, lifted his arms and slapped his thighs, and ambled toward the field. When she had first met him, he always kept his head down. He confessed to her that he was in perpetual despair. He went on at length about *The Wedding of Burgher van Dam,* the somber couple in dark clothing standing at attention in the chandelier-lit chamber, the crystal rosary hanging on a finial, each bead minutely reflecting the room, with its chair, table, mirror, and a door opening onto a garden where a bird sat on a fruit-laden branch, and plowed fields stretched out beyond a low wall. He showed her the gargoyles, hidden in the furniture as in a child's puzzle, glaring down on the union. James lived in this world of minute, enveloping detail, immersed in art, and could reveal all of this to her. (How she loved men to teach her things! Here she had put her hand on his; they sat side by side on her sofa, thighs touching, the book open on their laps.) And yet he was miserable. She had looked helplessly up at him through her lashes; she moistened her lips and parted them. Yes, he would do. "You are destined to be great," she whispered. She rescued him, built him up, encouraged him (really, Mauritius was her idea — she was the one with critical acuity — but he would harvest the fame), straightened his spine, told him to keep his head high. And now — who knows why? just to irk her, no doubt — there he was, shambling around, slumped. Why did he want to destroy all her hard work? Did he think he was better than she was? Why did he attack her like this? Why this exaggerated show of pain? So theatrical, and over nothing. He was the one who had pushed her away in bed. Dismissed from his mind the lunch she had been so eager to have with him. Oh, so very temperamental he was! And she was supposed to treat him with endless consideration and caution, while he trampled on her and with camp-counselor joviality brushed off her hurts as trifling. Have a glass of milk! Take a nap! You'll be fine tomorrow!

And yes — she lifted her foot and took herself up another step — Kuno was the same. For all he knew, she might be mortally ill, she might have a spot on her lung, and yet he had told her to go to her mother, whose constant manipulations, he very well knew, gave Melpomene ghastly headaches. She would lock herself away for a month, retool her factory, stop manufacturing his image. (As she ascended to the next step, the riser creaked.) She had to rescue herself; no one else would. She would go back to the city, find an important job — ethics; yes. A consultant to hospitals, corporations, and she would appear on television, and her insights would be quoted by other leaders. . . .

But she was nothing! Of course — she had forgotten.

The doorknobs were cold, the pompous crystal doorknobs that been the inspiration of his first wife, blond, domineering, and spoiled. If Melpomene couldn't keep James — suppose he found her out! — then she couldn't keep anyone. People merely tolerated her. A loathsome creature with slack breasts, a shriveled womb, a harpy's face. She had to wait, to say sweet things, to be tender. God help her if she spilled the truth. The world would crack apart.

Fatefully she walked along the hall. If music were to accompany this moment, a fugue would now build and build. Gabriel was right: you had to invent a story. Would she get the gun? Or would she retrieve James? If Kuno was nothing but a gigantic No, then she had only James. She couldn't survive alone.

She would swim far out in the icy, deep water (now framed by the window, blood-colored, black in the hollows between the swells) and patiently bring him back. Slave away.

No, this was self-pity and must be stopped. James was easy, eager to please her, his round eyes bright, his arms open, given to whistling absentminded bursts of Brahms or Schubert. (James and his Romantics. She, being more efficient, wanted to hear only Bach, because Bach surpassed all the rest.) Dear James. The night they met, when she absorbed his heated, unpatrolled gaze, her first thought had been, I can do with this one what I please. Even though Kuno had been at her side, James had rushed on about Georges de La Tour, and the two men had subtly dueled. Kuno dismissed Georges de La Tour as being contrived in his effects, comparable to painting on velvet. And the next day James sent her a big, lavish book, paintings at the Louvre. After her previous husband — he had mysteriously turned aloof and watchful with her, and their parting had been mild, finally — and after the unreliable though potent Kuno, James was a relief.

Oh, Lord, what torments Kuno devised for her. Yes, he would spend the entire day of her birthday with her, beginning at sunrise, and yes, he would take her to dinner at the best of restaurants (of course he knew the owner), and yes, he would take her back to his place for a lovely surprise, a gift she had always wanted. But then he forgot. Or perhaps he never intended to see her, and had only made promises when she provoked his guilt. But James — somehow he found out about the empty day she was doomed to spend alone, and he appeared with pink roses and a lapis lazuli necklace, and he took her to see the last Mauritius in private hands, in the mansion of a crone. *The Instruction of the Virgin* or some such. Melpomene gazed at the simple profile of a beautiful young woman next to a candle, an open book in her hands, and told James that was all she wanted to be. A month later, he gave her a diamond necklace that had belonged to his grandmother. (Perhaps now was the moment to sell it. The interest on her capital was not all that lavish.)

He didn't care about the study. Books and papers and trays of slides sat around in messy stacks rather than on the shelves. Despite his wish to destroy the place, it was still evident she had done a good job here: the rosewood furniture, the best equipment (donated by a fellowship member who was retiring from his law practice), her photograph in a silver frame, the Mauritius reproduction ordered at exorbitant cost from the Rijksmuseum. And yet he refused to respect her gifts. He refused to work. Just to spite her. At least he kept the Venetian leather diary out on his desk and had not yet set a cup of coffee on it.

She listened. The phone was ringing in her study below. She looked around. James was still outside. She sat down. The binding on the diary crackled when she opened it; the pages were blank. How dare he! All that money she'd spent, and on the special pen with a gold nib, too, just for writing on this excellent paper.

Now what was it she had been searching for? It was imperative that she find it, but what was it? What was her story? She had awakened happy. James had cast her aside. Her mother had called. Kuno had forced her to wait and had told her to go to her mother. James had abandoned her. Her headache had expanded and deepened. People with complaints had come and gone. (The dark, flawed feeling returned again.) She had lain down in the cemetery. Gabriel, unimpressed, had left abruptly. She had slowly climbed the stairs, her heart aching. The music had been ominous as she walked along the hall. . . .

She opened a drawer. He probably kept the thing wrapped in a sock. She wanted only to feel the cold metal against her temple, to memorize that sensation. As a memento mori. To proclaim: This is how far I have come. And at that exact moment Kuno might arrive. Silently she would regard him over her shoulder as if to say, See what you have driven me to do?

The computer screen shed a green phosphorescence in the twilit room. BANK TAXES MAURIT ALICE. Alice.

Now she heard the muffled rhythms of Kuno's voice on her answering machine. Good. Let him suffer. Interesting that even with the thick carpet she had put down here, voices still carried from below. Perhaps James made a habit of eavesdropping on her; perhaps he knew. . . . No, nothing penetrated that skull.

Alice. Not a name Melpomene recognized, and through skillful probing she had learned the names and predilections of all his former women and the exact extent of his attraction to them. Of course her overscrupulousness would ordinarily never permit her to eavesdrop or to intrude on his files or his mail. But today was different. No — she was just giving herself excuses. On the other hand, this was an emergency. She would be putting a gun to her head in the next few minutes, so what did her actions matter? Well, they would matter to God, wouldn't they? If He existed, and He must, but far away, in a marble chamber, completely uninterested in her, dozing. Really, it was a case of self-defense. Tomorrow she might find herself in the bus terminal, lugging her belongings around in shopping bags. And if he had spied on her. . . . She could prove before a board of ethicists why it was absolutely necessary — urgent, in fact — to call ALICE out of the depths of the computer. Wouldn't each of you, she would say, appealing to them, wouldn't each of you do just what I did? It looks like snooping, but what would you do if you loved him and he was about to ruin his life and yours? I'm no worse than anyone else. Christ said, Do not judge. Well, you must not judge *me*. You must view me with love in your hearts. It was not as if she were tearing open an envelope and reading a secret letter. And hadn't James invited her to use the computer? Anyway, ALICE might be a monster, a ruthless leech like his first wife, out to scare James, to blackmail him. Melpomene's plan to revive and transform James had failed thus far. By reading ALICE she would find out what was wrong with him, and so she would better be able to help him. She was morally compelled to do this, even though she was hard-pressed and weary, and had to keep pushing herself so that other thoughts, so that self-condemnation, didn't win out and drown her, and, besides, an ocean thundered inside her head.

The far edge of the bay darkened, a spark tossing up on the waters here and there. Iron tendrils of cloud turned black. Veils of fog, caught in the failing light, blew past. From now on, nights would be bitter; from now on, the air, smelling of woodsmoke, would be colder than the water, and more fogs would appear; and then the water would also grow cold. The harvest was finished; the field was nothing now but straw smelling of decay, humps of brown earth here and there. Nothing could ever grow here again. A few icy drops struck his cheek. A twinge pierced his jaw. Spending the night out here roaming like a dispossessed ghost was a ridiculous gesture. He headed toward the house. There's been a misunderstanding, he would say. And the pearls — he would get out the pearls.

Dear Alice, dearest Alice,
  I'm a fool. You'll think it strange that I'm writing you. But I still feel in contact with you. I always will. You often appear in my

dreams. *We embrace, we kiss, and it's the same as ever. There's no one I've had a deeper connection with. I still feel I can tell you things I've never told anyone else. How long has it been since we last said goodbye, on the street corner? Once I saw you after that going down the steps of the museum, but you didn't see me. You were with some others. I almost went up to you. Today I was studying Mauritius's* Girl Bathing. *You were the first person to reveal that painting to me, to make me see Mauritius. You said his work contained a profound message. I didn't understand you very well then, but I'm beginning to now. I've been trying to start a book about him and I keep wondering what you would say, how you might help. I need to do something serious. Ever since we broke up, if that's what we did, I haven't accomplished much of anything. I have been living a false life. I wanted to tell you that I saw for the first time that she wasn't looking over her shoulder in mild surprise, as I'd always thought, as if the painter had startled her in the act of sponging her throat. No, nothing surprises her. She knows — that's why she's holding up the white cloth to her bosom. She's beckoning, and her eyes are full of light. What is Mauritius trying to convey here? I feel that I know, but that I can't locate the knowledge. I think she's seen everything. She has a secret; she must keep silent. Perhaps the secret is the painting hanging on the wall behind her head. You once pointed out to me that it was a garden. A painting is a machine for entering eternity. I wanted to tell you that, Alice, dearest Alice.*

The fact is that even after all this time I can't forget you. This morning I dreamed that I was in a building that had paintings on the wall (it was a direct experience: there were no labels in my brain and so I didn't think of the place as a museum or gallery), and I could enter the paintings, like Alice (!) going through the looking glass. Like passing through the wall of an aquarium. I could actually feel my skin, my body, passing through an invisible barrier. And then you appeared. I've never stopped loving you. Probably you don't want to hear that. Probably you're very happy with someone else and still angry at me for what I did. But in the dream the love I felt for you was overwhelming, more real than my life as I sit here writing you. Whenever I'm in your old neighborhood, I hope I'll run into you even though you probably haven't been there in years. I want to apologize. You have every reason to hate me. I didn't know what to do with my love for you. It was inconvenient, out of control, it didn't fit in. I was frightened. I married someone else when it was obvious that you should have been the one. And when that marriage collapsed, as you probably knew it would, an affair I was having immediately turned into my second marriage. I don't even know why. Well, she's been a good influence, I think. I don't know what's happened to me, Alice. It's as if I've been asleep all these years and woke up only today. Dearest Alice, I hope you won't mind this letter. It's all right if you laugh at me, or despise me. I still love you. I'm well, and I very much hope that you are, too, but suppose that one of us has a heart attack or dies in a plane crash. Then our lives will have ended without this wound between us ever healing, without your knowing how I feel in my soul. You are the only person who would understand about the secret, the beckoning, the garden. When I lay next to you that last time, I put my hand on your collarbone, and suddenly I could sense your body as if it were my own. Never have I been as close to anyone else. I beg you: Let me see you, just once. Oh, Alice, the times we were together, the unexpected beauty, the most

The house was dark and silent. When he switched on the bathroom light, he startled himself. Bowing his head as he washed his hands, he turned his eyes to the mirror. The top of his head had become gray, and there was a pink spot in the center. Just like that! Oh, Melpomene had teased him about a strand here and there, but now, here on the crown, where no one could see, he had grown old. He had gone running down to the bay this morning to play, the last free morning before school started, and this afternoon he had followed the wrack line, and now he was old. He reached for one of the linen guest towels but withdrew his hands and dried them on his pants.

He would give everything up. His loves were finished. Rain spattered the windows. In her study the phone rang. He went into the chilly sun-room, stepped over stacks of books he was planning to read, and sank into the leather reclining chair. (Melpomene had given it to him after some old lover had returned it.) The sun, a disk of purple behind a black cloud, dropped into the bay, leaving the air a grainy indigo.

Freedom, he would say to her. If we don't have that. . . .

Melpomene, the woman he had thought was all his, might refuse him; she might have another lover. (The ripple coursed through his gut again.) And it was true that James was worthless, that no exceptions would be made on his behalf, that good fortune directed itself to other men but not to him, that he was just an assemblage of protoplasm, a means by which certain acids replicated themselves down through the eons, but at least he could read a book. Nature, so busy with murder, had scarcely taken writing into account; she was too myopic to notice the hidden messages passed down the generations, the secret exchange of knowledge, the escape that books offered from time and space and death. He had inherited a big library, and Melpomene also had thousands of books; the house contained at least a million realms. All other men might outstrip him, laugh at him, destroy him (the date of the execution had been set; he just didn't know when it would take place), but he could meanwhile read Epictetus.

His breathing slowed, he became dreamily attentive, he ceased consciously to see the words, and a fine mist rose from the page and seeped into his brainpan, forming pictures.

What makes the tyrant formidable? — The guards, you say, and their swords, and the men of the bedchamber, and those who exclude persons who would enter. (Men in togas and helmets; pillared marble halls.) *— Why, then, is it that, if you bring a child into the presence of the tyrant while he is with his guards, the child is not afraid?* (A boy with an open face and thin arms.) . . . If only he could live alone with his books, safe from love, from terror.

A gift would divert and calm her, and the pearl necklace seemed right, though he could never be certain. His first gift to her, a necklace of lapis lazuli to match her eyes, had taken him a long time to find. She had drawn it out of its velvet box as if grasping the tail of a venomous snake. Other gifts of his she had barely glanced at. But obviously she wanted and admired certain objects. Early in their courtship, when he was about to fly to Amsterdam, she set her jewelry chest on the bed and showed him gold chains and diamond pins, describing the lovers who had given them to her, occasionally remarking, "And even today he's one of the dearest people in my life" or "I'm still utterly fond of him." He postponed the trip; his research could wait. She owned so much clothing that he had extra closets built for her in the garage. She bought herself whatever she pleased. When they had been secret lovers, she would whirl around in a new dress and ask him what he thought. But she would never tell him what she wanted. He was supposed to guess.

Alice was the sort of woman who was happy with a pocket knife, a flashlight. But when Melpomene told him she was terrified of a thief in the night who would rape and kill her, and James gave her a flashlight to keep on her night table, she turned pale, set her jaw, and he never saw the present again. Alice. Where could she be living now? Her old block in the city, her rented carriage house set in a garden, was now the site of an office building. How would he find her address? But even if he did, he wouldn't send the letter he'd begun today. No. His words to her were like his performance in bed with Melpomene — pathetic. Alice would never know. She would grow old and never know what he still felt.

He read until his eyelids drooped. The lines on the page swam. Water flickered, a great pale expanse of it, and in the shadowy distance rose a golden city with white plumes — sailing ships. The lights on the waves rippled toward him, bits of green flashing. Suddenly a big green square of light exploded, jolting him. Where was he? He was thinking in a foreign language, surrounded by people he knew well but who remained obstinately strange. He was not in his bed. Years had passed. The crown of his head was gray. All the lunging mirrors in the house attested to that.

Fog blurred the hedgerow into a wall and hid the tops of the trees. The field had faded to a depleted, ancient dun. The rain shook a pair of dried pods that hung at the tip of a catalpa branch. He blinked, and the air became slightly more opaque than it had been a second earlier. Geese cried overhead. The window panes gave off a cool breath. A film dropped over the pages of the book. Objects in the room dissolved and sank.

Ten

RAIN BLEW against the windows. Priscilla sat on the sofa looking up at the Reverend in her chair. A truncated cone of yellow light from the desk lamp glinted in the watery, speckled square of the mirror just above the her head and glazed the photographs of the Reverend, on a beach, smiling up at the governor; the Reverend with the anthropologist Ruth Victor (the Reverend had promised Priscilla that one day Ruth Victor would visit and Priscilla could meet her); the Reverend, her posture queenly, addressing an ecumenical gathering in the Doge's Palace; the Reverend in a garden holding a bouquet of roses and standing arm in arm with a tall, round-faced man, his eyes squeezed shut — wasn't that Mr. Gilman? Priscilla had glimpsed him at services, usually sitting at the far end of the front row, nodding slightly or gazing up in satisfaction at the Reverend. He stayed in the background; he was some sort of scholar, well-off, elegant in his tailored suits. A splendid marriage, according to all Priscilla could make out from talks the Reverend had delivered about spouses as the guardians of each other's solitude; two companionable swans, side by side, tolerant, affectionate, intelligent.

Priscilla herself had not succeeded in being married even once, and yet again she was here in the study crying, a tremendous gnawing in her chest; how she had loved that man — for years! — but when she had been with him, as the Reverend had charitably pointed out, she had destroyed everything. Only the Reverend knew her secret.

"I tracked down his address. I have his phone number. I can hardly think of anything else. If I stopped thinking about him, I'd stop breathing. But if I went to him —"

"Oh, go to him," Melpomene murmured. She rubbed her temples. Her rage. Her head. That absurd, sentimental letter James had written — the nerve! In front of her lay the open Bible; she still had not composed her talk; the garden — what garden?; the country of the morning was ten thousand miles from here; the time kept going, going. Oh, how that angel galled her; she would stick it in the garage. How boorish of Gabriel Porter to refuse her largesse. If Kuno weren't so extraordinarily stingy, he would have given her some of his paintings and she wouldn't have to rely on corrupt reproductions.

"What?"

"You've been talking about him forever," Melpomene said irritably. "About once a month you come to ask me about this, and it's always the same story. You dream about him, you worry about him. You ought to call him up right now. *Tell* him you had his child. He'll be thrilled. Here. Call him right now. What's his number?"

"But I couldn't just —"

"You couldn't just?"

"It's — it's long distance." She flushed. Actually talk to him? No — impossible.

"I'll pay for the call." Melpomene picked up the receiver. Oh, you are the busy authority, she said to herself. Aren't you having a wonderful time, with your headache and your unfaithful men and your clichés and your platitudes and your wrinkled face and your packed theater! You know so much; you tell everyone what to do; but you are finished. Even in this backwater, you're a nobody. You ought to shoot yourself in the head. But then her mouth, her lovely mouth would be ruined, and in death she wanted Kuno to kiss her. Pills, then. Behind the Jerusalem Bible. Deep sleep. God is not dead nor doth he sleep. "Tell me the number. Right now, Priscilla."

The Reverend's face was pale, her eyes hectic, her voice rasping. Priscilla held her knees as if the room itself had abruptly tilted and she were about to lose her balance. "I'm just worried," she mumbled.

"What? Don't be afraid. We don't need to call him. Better yet — I'll drive you. Yes, why not? Where does he live? I don't mind how far it is. Let's go." The Reverend stood up. An electrical field emanated from her form, and her blood-less face drew Priscilla out of her chair. "We'll go in my wonderful car — he'll be very impressed. I'd loan you my sable, but it's still in storage. And you should wear a beauti-ful dress — white, so that he'll think of marriage. But low-cut. 'The Kingdom of the Father is spread upon the earth and men do not see it.' I'll go in first and speak to him, and I'll tell him you love him, you've only ever loved him of all the men, that he is the most important, the most profound connection you have in the universe, that in the presence of your own death you've seen what is essential to you, and that is to go to him, *go to him,* and if he doesn't understand then he's nothing but an insect."

"But I don't think I — are you — are you making fun of me?"

"You love him. Why else live? Let's go."

"This is craz———" Priscilla broke off and stared at the tumbled fringe of the tree-of-life carpet. "I have to leave —"

"No, don't," Melpomene said quietly. She listened to her own breath and felt the sharp edge of the writing table against her palm. She squeezed her hand until she felt pain. She was in control. Yes, she could see everything. Very clearly. "I think something important is happening here, after all this wasted time, and I do mean wasted."

"But it's after seven. My boy — I have to pick him up from orchestra rehearsal. He'll be waiting, and the storm is supposed to get worse."

The roar of the rain on the roof, on the windows, formed a temple around them. They stood facing each other under a single great vertical arch, both of them surprised and fearful, as if a third person, a marauder, had entered the room and they had to be extremely cautious. Priscilla backed toward the door.

The Reverend smiled with exceptional sweetness, and her voice grew warm and soft. "I wanted to push you a little so that you could get a glimpse of your fantasy. I used a strategem to break you out of your habitual thinking. You know that what I want for you more than anything is peace and understanding, and if I have to drag you — drag you by your hair out of hell, I will."

"Oh," said Priscilla. "I — I know that, and I'm so thankful. But I really do have to pick up my boy. Can I come back on your next visitors' day?"

The Reverend sat down at her desk and stroked a page of the open Bible with her fingertips. So tired. "Do what you want." She glanced at her watch and at the answering machine, with its red light, blinking because Kuno, nervous and uncertain, was trapped inside, begging to be released. "You're free."

You could be walking along the shore, and suddenly all the water would retreat, and the seabed, with its mud and rocks and wilted vegetation, would be exposed for miles, and you might even think it was fun to walk out there, and then a wall of water the height of a tall building would come thundering toward you, and suck you far out into the ocean, where the bottom was miles below your flailing feet, and the waves would close over your head, and you would be twisted by the violent current, and the breath knocked out of your chest and replaced with saltwater. And you would be completely alone, and no one could save you. Perhaps he didn't even know that you went out to walk along the shore. Perhaps no one knew how it happened to you, and afterward they would find your swollen corpse.

"Please, I need to see you. Please." Kristen, very faint. Ah, only Kristen, not anyone who would love Melpomene or help her or heal her. No one who would sympathize with her about James's awful betrayal. Poor, dear Kristen. If only she knew how much she and Melpomene were alike. Kristen: squarely in the light, untouched by evil, completely vulnerable.

Melpomene started to look up the number of the psychiatrist. But wait — her voice might shake. Collect yourself or he'll see you for the fraud you are. He already condescends to you. Think. If there's one thing you excel at, it's thinking. Categorize.

1. Kuno had abandoned her. 2. A tremendous weight hung over her head — what was it? Upstairs, in James's study, in James's computer. ALICE. Melpomene had gone there for the gun and had found ALICE instead. Oh, her fury; she had to will herself to leave the room before something got smashed. Perhaps James had already given his money to this woman, perhaps he would be discarding Melpomene in a matter of days. (Fortunately, she had packed a suitcase.) Do me a favor, she would say. Cut off my head, too. 3. And somewhere around, if he had not already fulfilled his schemes and deceptions and gone to the woman, if he had not been mangled in a bloody accident on the highway, was James himself, the man who had bound himself to her with sacred ties and who had yawned at her in bed this morning, right after her bad dream about the beast.

All right, then, these conditions predominated. What solution for them? The most economical, the neatest? Well, simply to put her arm around him and say, You seem to have a problem here. You've gone around today with a face like a fiend, and I'm worried about you. I'm extremely overburdened, but let's talk.

He would have to come to her, though. If she left her office she would go upstairs, get the gun, or James's exquisitely sharp razor — no, the pills, hidden right here. But her mouth was utterly dry. And first, she would have to pour gasoline around and she would have to burn the house down. So the fellowship would mourn it as a tragic accident and not lose faith.

Afraid, she was wrenchingly afraid now. The remedy was ruthlessness. She had to take herself in hand. Yes, you are fat and old and disgusting. You are nothing, an empty shell. Kristen — Kristen, helpless, truly loved Melpomene, but really she loved some imaginary Reverend, and the person she actually longed for was Gabriel. (Without all the hair and jewelry he might be rather erotic. And he liked French poetry. She could make something of him, but she had no more energy to give.) You're really something, aren't you? Clinging to the inept, the confused, the needy, putting everyone before yourself. Oh, her cross was that her love was overpowering; no one could take it. She ought to have her heart cut out. But they were cutting it out of her, a little at a time; they were pushing her under the waves.

She could objectively view all these thoughts, each biting the tail of the next, because she was lucid. She even possessed a touch of the divine; certainly God had announced Himself to her more than once since that day in Notre-Dame.

Night had come. Between now and sleep, the time was unstructured; it could flow in any number of dangerous directions.

Let the lovers wander hand in hand through flowering meadows, let them walk, arms around each other, along the shore. Let them die of cancer. She sank her teeth into the fleshy part of her thumb, breaking the skin. She would stay here; she would starve to death.

*

Rain clicked on the gutters, and the wind sent drafts through the room, stirring the curtains. Another day over. Capstones had been put on arches, symphonies scored, paintings finished, new particles discovered, love consummated millions of times. But he had done virtually nothing. Others, far more fortunate, had won prizes, had carried off beautiful women. And where was his gold watch, his gleaming trophy, his priceless wisdom, awarded simply because he had survived? (Walking on the sides of his feet as noiselessly as an Indian brave, he went upstairs.) Only in recent human history had people lived past the age of thirty-five. Nature was finished with him now. . . . If only he'd been born elsewhere — in some land where you followed certain rituals and did what your father had done and otherwise were not responsible for manufacturing your own life and keeping it in motion and inventing reasons to go on.

The bathwater was too hot, and he had to run cold water and stir it with his hand before he could step in. In the tub, a hot cloth over his eyes, he would vanish; the day would not have happened. The water was so deep that he almost floated. Gently lifted, he rubbed a bar of soap across his belly. There she had stroked him this morning — was it the morning of this same day? They had lain in bed; he had dreamed; her hair a forest; their promised intimacy was absolute and certain; he knew she wanted him to get up and begin his work, to be a man.

Before their marriage, she had said, "Ask me any question and I will tell you the truth." Her truth was that he was the only man she loved, had ever really loved, she was finished with the others, she was gambling everything on him. This was her final marriage. She wanted to evolve toward a more luminous knowledge; one could develop, become great. Since childhood she had dreamed of triumphs of every sort. She now invoked Plato, Buddha, the Gospels, St. Teresa of Avila, Thoreau, Nietzsche. All the thinkers he had discarded after his adolescence. "I promise always to be completely honest with you, and if you're honest with me, together we'll advance." A new idea to him: rather than simply being married, they would be actively engaged in a project that amounted to nothing less than the transmutation of their souls. Their marriage would be founded on the granite of mutual truth and something she called commitment (this was a popular word and suggested some internal operation that he did not yet know how to perform, since it didn't seem to involve more love or attention or fidelity, but rather an activity familiar to other husbands and lovers that transcended all those things). Both had made horrible mistakes in the past, had fallen for phantoms, had played vacuous roles; now they would be pure.

"What do you want most?" she asked, her gaze as wide as the sky.

He refused to say.

"You can tell me. I will accept with all my heart whatever you say. Nothing can change my love for you."

He replied: "The first thing that comes to mind is that I'd like to live alone in a library that contained an art museum, something like the library of Lorenzo de' Medici in Florence. And I could really understand what I read and what art was. And I could listen to all the music I like. I'd wish for the solitude to do all those things."

She laughed, and he was relieved.

"What kind of life is that?" She laughed again, fully and

with complete confidence. "What kind of life is that — without me? I don't exist? Just your books? Then goodbye!" Her voice took on an edge. "You'll turn into one of those cranky old men, pottering around in a filthy sweatshirt and talking to yourself."

Oh, but what he'd really intended was that she of course would share his solitude. By "alone" he had meant, removed from the tedious social life his first wife had perpetuated, with her constant invasions and interruptions. Melpomene had smiled.

Running cold water, he splashed himself and thought of that expression, so full of interest, so vibrant — one he yearned to see again. But why had she smiled at just that moment? Could it be that she was thinking she was going to win after all? That she had outmaneuvered and defeated him? Had it been simply a game all along?

His skin and hair and clothes were clean. A trio of Jameses appeared in the panes of the bay window. The stove clock flashed its numbers: 7:22! Fewer than five hours left of the day!

Too late to start something new. He shook his head, and the reflections shook theirs. Mauritius loved to paint the reflections of people — in water, in windows slightly ajar, in goblets, in jars of preserved fruit, in crystal beads. To accomplish some of his effects he must have used not only the camera obscura but also an ingenious arrangement of mirrors. At any rate only his back is ever portrayed; in *Tavern Scene,* you see his broad cavalier's hat with its plume; his long fingers confidently holding up a brush as if it were a baton, announcing: I know how to work, I will reveal my thought. And always in the foreground a heavy curtain, decorated with vines and flowers, that has been pulled aside to reveal an inner room with a mirror reflecting a doorway, and, sometimes, a chamber beyond that, distant and yet near. A simple room, viewed in such a moment of stillness, revealed the strangeness of the most ordinary places and moments. What could be more remarkable or mysterious than this momentary kitchen and the man with the sad demeanor standing and looking out a bay window at nothing but darkness and his own scattered images?

The drumming of the rain was deafening. He would find Alice and tell her these thoughts. Tall and bosomy and leggy and dark-eyed, and she was sensuous without even knowing it. Melpomene flirted until all the attention in a room was pulled toward her. Every move seemed conscious. Once she had playfully shown him how she could even sob at will; it was a matter of choking off her breathing and heaving her chest, and soon the sobs came of themselves, and then the tears. Perhaps his love for Alice was only imagined. (It was his first wife, and his mother, and the friends he had then who had insisted on the marriage, on his giving up Alice. As far as he could recall, Alice had never asked him for anything.) But here he was — after how many years? — thinking of her, desiring her. His three reflections were pensive. They were thinking of fragments of a person they didn't know, a few colored, enticing bits. Alice remained in the past, fixed in some occluded substance.

But the immediate world was here: the pressure of the air, the chill that stiffened his fingers, the click of Melpomene's study door making a hot, crowded sensation surge through his chest. (Oh, God, she was coming!)

He waited. Perhaps Melpomene wanted him to go to her. Perhaps the opening of the door was a summons. But no, he heard her voice; she must be speaking on the telephone or chatting with a visitor, and a sudden draft must have pushed the door ajar.

She would have to come out to eat; as far as he knew, she hadn't had anything all day. And she needed something restorative. A food that would make her happy, that would satisfy her at last, as she had yet to be genuinely satisfied with anything he had done. He had never pointed that out to her. The list of matters he had not pointed out had now grown very long. It extended all the way across the lawn and into the woods, where the leaves, under panels of yellow cast by the windows, shook in the wet darkness. Had his own wish to compromise, to keep her peaceful, damaged his integrity?

Soon they would both be old. The transparent ribbons of their lives would rise up and disappear. He was aging by the second. The stove clock said so. She, too, would run out of seconds; so many had already been used up. And yet the woman held the delicate golden balance, the pans empty, and even if there were no Judgment Day and all we had was this instant, right now, everything had to matter — everything. Today might be his last chance. He would dissuade her from going away, if that was what she had been discussing so eagerly on the phone this morning. What would become of her out there? Night and storms and highways terrified her. He would beg her; he would prove his love. She had set up the test; so far he had failed. Following his own desire, rooted in the body's wish to survive, he had eaten without waiting for her, and because of this trivial thing she believed she had been forsaken. Deliberately hurt. So she claimed. But was that really true? Perhaps he loved no one.

He sharpened a knife and began to cut up potatoes and carrots and onions. What else could he do? And when everything was weighed, at the end, on his deathbed, this would probably be the important thing to remember about this day: he had made soup.

Silence. The talking had stopped. Was Melpomene all right? Had she run away? In the past she had frightened him by describing her attraction to the straightedge razor, to his grandfather's gun. Curious that these matters refused to stay in his mind. When he tried to reason with her, to suggest that she see a doctor, she became vicious (she knew better than anyone that doctors only wanted money and were morons besides; she was forever being forced to clean up the messes psychiatrists made). And if he seemed to be watching her too closely, if he insisted that she rest and eat, she became more agitated and withdrew — she ran away for a few hours or locked herself in her study or in their bedroom. A day or so later, she would beam at him. "See how happy I am?" she would exclaim, smiling and radiant and alluring. "You see that I'm calm, that I'm not immersed. I'm very happy, very, very, very happy!" How could he forget how she really was, the constant danger that awaited her? And yet he did, again and again, because she was thoroughly rational as well.

He could phone Ruth for advice. Perhaps she could come for the weekend; she was good-humored and helpful. But Melpomene considered Ruth incapable of genuine sympathy. "You're so naive, James, if you think Ruth is any kind of real friend to you or to me. One time when I was very low I called her, and she told me to see a professional! As if I didn't know exactly myself, as a professional, what was going on. She's not someone you ought to trust."

He put down the knife and stepped into the corridor. Melpomene's door was still ajar. She stood before her desk, her chin down, her profile illuminated by the muted amber light. He quietly approached. She tensed but did not move.

Her prettiness pleased him, and he longed to touch her skin. He was about to kiss her, his lips an inch from her face, when she turned to him, her eyes full of wrath and cunning. "Hello, dear," she said very amiably.

It was then that James saw the policeman. In his black leather, he had nearly merged with the shadows. James was stricken with a stupefying thought: she had discovered that the seashell was missing from her drawer and had reported it. "Excuse me," James said, withdrawing, heart pounding.

"Officer Finley here — Sam" — her arpeggio laugh came spilling out — "is telling me how happy the police are about our project over at the bus terminal."

"You've sure been good for the community, Reverend," the policeman said. He kept his eyes on the floor. Reared by nuns, no doubt. "People are grateful."

"That is indeed the case," James said, realizing how absurd his reaction was but still uneasy. The policeman was young and handsome; was he the one? They were drinking out of tiny glasses.

"Well, I'll get back to making dinner. Sorry to interrupt."

"Oh, darling, of course it's all right. But you must be starving. Run along, then. You know how you get when you don't eat. You ought to have a glass of milk right away.

He has a delicate constitution, Sam, and I have to take very good care of him."

He answered the phone in the kitchen. It was Melpomene's mother.

"How are you doing?" he asked, a little too robustly.

"Oh, I'm fine, I'm fine," she said. "I hope I'm not bothering you — you're not having dinner, are you?"

"Oh, not at all — just fixing some soup. So — you're fine?"

"Has Melpomene left yet? I need to ask her something."

"Ah, well. I think she's with someone at the moment. Can she call you back?"

"She's still at the house — she's not coming?"

"Well, she's had a busy day. I'll have her call you."

"I don't want to bother her anymore. Tell her that I've hidden all my jewelry in the toes of my shoes in the bedroom closet."

"I don't understand. What do you mean?"

"She'll know. Goodbye, James. Get back to your cooking. She's lucky to have you."

Odd that she should say that; Melpomene had always maintained that her mother felt she should have married someone more dynamic.

It was a soup that he had been given as a small child when he was traveling with his family. Had they been on the deck of an ocean liner? Or in a restaurant in Paris, with the prow of the Île furrowing the Seine? Men in long white aprons served the soup. Hot, subtly flavored, exactly what his body needed. Had he been feverish? To this day in any restaurant, he always ordered the soup, and had almost forgotten why; a silly thing; a buried hope that he would again find the food that alone was the correct one for him; its molecules, fulfilling their destiny, would flow to his bones and blood and brain and render him happy and whole again as he had been made on that chill, misty day with his mother at his side.

Melpomene would come out of the study and see the delicious meal on the dining table and everything else would be erased. The scallop shell was again nestled under the lace and satin. She was justified in her anger when he entered her study without knocking. (He'd have to explain that the noise of the rain drowned out the sound of the police car, the wind had blown the door open, and he had assumed she was alone.) Although she seldom forgot what was done to her, she easily forgot what she had done to others, and her own previous moods as well. His accumulation of grievances astonished him; a part of his brain had been recording her wrongs all along.

The gale made the house shudder, and the rain obliterated everything except the hiss of the vegetables as he stirred them in the pan and added broth. Yes, he could survive alone. He spent most of each day in isolation. Gradually he had learned to cook and to run the household. Without his being aware, she had taught him not to depend on her, and that was something. All his life he had been afraid of loneliness; he had waited for women to bring him food and had been upset when they failed him. When Melpomene cooked, her movements were hasty and impatient. Whenever she felt obliged to invite the board members for dinner, she boiled vegetables until they were limp and pale, she roasted meat until it was dry, she prepared thick gravies, all the while complaining about the time being wasted. It was work to eat her food, and the work was doubled by the obligation to praise it as well as her sacrifices. For an interval, he'd tried taking her, and anyone she felt she ought to entertain, to restaurants. She liked that well enough, but she hated the expense, and lately his invitations for them to dine out alone seemed only to annoy her.

But she did love (or had once loved) getting out the best china and silver and linen, and running into the dining room with trays of demitasses, exhaling audibly to show her pleasure, performing skillfully at every turn. And at the beginning, she had wanted to cook for him. She promised him exquisite cuisine. Ruth had told him about legendary dinners Melpomene had produced, in particular about one that had inspired a distinguished chef to murmur, "The Lord's gain is our loss."

And Alice. Alice used to pass her hands over a potato, an onion, a piece of cheese, and turn them into wonderful meals. Of course it was forbidden to evaluate a woman by her cooking; the fists of many women would hammer him for that. But he was free, was he not, to think privately of a lovely woman — no woman in particular — with long, sweet-smelling hair, wearing a diaphanous dress and floating through a polished, flower-bedecked room to bring him a delicious platter she had happily prepared? And she would put her soft hands on either side of his face, and he would press his face to her breast. . . . •

The soup was bubbling. He went to the window. The police car was nowhere to be seen. A figure in the drive was dragging a suitcase through the downpour. The trunk of Melpomene's car sprang open. James hurried toward the door. Perhaps she really intended to go to her mother. Perhaps it was true that her mother was suicidal; impossible to tell. Or maybe Melpomene would drive around for an hour or two and then come back and ask him to observe how very, very happy she was. He stopped in the vestibule and searched for an umbrella. But why the heavy suitcase? She was leaving for good.

The house without her: he would have solitude; he would have a rest from vigilance. But of course the remainder of his life would be destroyed.

That first night when he had seen her at the dinner table, her face lambent in the candlelight, he had imagined that he would eventually reach her depths. But the real Melpomene remained blackness and stars, hidden even from herself. (He winced at his own romanticism.) What did she want? She strove again and again for her own disappointment. What ever would please her? She seemed driven always to want something this world could not give her.

Gusts began to rattle the rain against the panes and shingles. It was turning to sleet. His heart was thumping, he was sweaty with fear, but he remained motionless in the dank vestibule, face pressed to the window silvered with water, watching the headlights. (*I hope you die.*) This time he would not go after her. He returned to the kitchen and stirred the soup, and cleaned the counter and threw away the peelings, and in the garbage pail he found the broken cup and plate.

Kuno discovered that he had a great many things to do as soon as he unlocked the door to his place. This barbarous country: everything new and yet broken. And Janine had demanded to have dinner with him immediately. In Paris he had thought not of her but of Melpomene. Conducted long conversations with Mel in his head as he paced through the Louvre day after day. During an organ concert at Notre-Dame he remembered her experience there (something similar had happened to him years ago at Chartres — the wish to work for the glory of something greater than himself; to exert himself for something besides fame and money). He longed to curl up at her side; with her, edges grew more defined, colors brighter, textures more inflected. The only moments when he had truly felt safe and well were in her arms; she was a piece of elusive light. Shouting to her over the feeble phone connection from the plane and hearing, after a pause in which the words were tossed up to a satellite and down again, her faint, honeyed voice, he had been lifted, as an infusion of medication can promptly stop pain. Worried that she might have already taken herself away — to some mountaintop or jungle, to one of those places she was always threatening to go — he was ready to hold her tightly and prevent her escape. Yet the woman with whom he had spoken on the phone after landing was alternately curt and wheedling, and his old nervousness returned. Yes, she was suffering; yes, her marriage was miserable; yes, she had used up that backwater; and he wanted to race to her, and assumed she would race to him. But then she brought up the overwhelming problem of her mother, poised with razor or pills in hand, and there was also her husband to consider. Yes, Kuno was disgustingly guilty of all the sins she heaped upon his head; he was even an insect, as she said; and there were — my God — thousands of other things to consider. And a million responsibilities of his own.

And he needed to sleep. He needed to lie in his own bed, in his own place, among his own things, and gently allow his eyes to close, his limbs to elongate. And wasn't it raining? And he had forgotten the comforting shape of his own pillow. But suppose she ran away, or harmed herself? Afraid, he sat up. He called her and got her machine. He left a message. He tried again and again, and left more messages. She might already have run away. How tired he was! No one worked harder than he did (that sheaf of little charcoal sketches he had done on the plane would probably bring several thousand). He'd call her tomorrow, or perhaps just show up — on Sunday at the church. (Once, in the early days, he'd threatened to kick her door down if she didn't open up. When she did, he jammed a bunch of roses in her hand and found her trembling with excitement.) Maybe not. Such an embarrassment, her insistence on being a minister. It didn't suit her. But she needed all those people needing her. She loved to dress up and stand in front of an awestruck congregation. The few times he'd visited, he found himself hating all the people who crowded around her at the church door.

And now this storm. Driving in the rain to meet her someplace — that inn she'd chosen off in the woods — would have been too difficult, and of course he didn't want her out in weather like this. She was a crazy driver, always getting speeding tickets or having minor accidents. Anyway, the flight, the argument with her, the dinner with Janine (and Janine's sulk when he didn't take her home), had all depleted him.

He would say that an important meeting with his dealer had come up as soon as he landed. Yes, the dealer was just leaving for Japan; someone wanted to buy Kuno's latest canvases, sight unseen. Good. Mel would be pleased. Later, if she asked, he would remember to reply that the buyer had welshed. There were no new paintings. He had done the sketches only because he thought he would be showing them to her. . . . Her hands and voice were so feminine and soothing that he felt as if he were lying on a grassy hill and a warm breeze were blowing. And she was always ready to remind him of the life of the spirit, to imbue him with hope. He knew her so well that they might be twins. She hadn't really meant those cutting things. Maybe they were for James, who had been endlessly cruel to her, and boring (this gave Kuno a bit of pleasure, as he ran his hand over his chest), or just part of the clouds and dust and waves she enjoyed stirring up. Meanwhile, he could see her face, elfin, peeking out at him from behind all that chaos and waving at him, signaling that she was just fine. Tomorrow he would see her. Or Sunday. He closed his eyes. His phone rang, far away, too far to reach.

She came up behind James and leaned her damp head against his back and cried. In the kitchen window he could see her form, tripartite, huddled, sketchy against the shreds of his own, the two of them mingled with the sleet and the shiny black and the shivering yellow leaves.

"I don't know how to live. . . . I don't know how to live. I just want to die."

"But — don't cry, please don't cry," he whispered, paralyzed. "But — of course you do. You're living right now. What is there to know? I love you. Everyone loves you. You're brilliant, you're impressive — like the man said, people are grateful —"

"Don't mock me. Don't talk down to me! Don't console

me! You're not my husband; you've never been my husband."

"What are you saying, darling? What?"

"I mean I want to know. I want to know myself." She sobbed. "And others. I want to learn. I don't want to cause any harm. I don't want to be bad. I'm interested in beauty, in truth. I want to be good. Is there any hope for me? What should I do?"

A surge of frozen rain shattered against the roof, the lawn, the trees; it seemed to have fallen from an immense distance, propelled from the icy center of the galaxy, where light itself was congealed in splashes.

Wir setzen uns mit Tränen nieder . . .

She had set the volume so that the choir and orchestra seemed to have stationed themselves in the dim living room, and the bass notes of the closing chorus of the St. Matthew Passion vibrated the windows. Ambushed by its beauty, he closed his eyes. The music swept through his bones and made him shiver; it completely possessed him.

She wept and sniffed. He opened his eyes. In the fireplace the ashes, dimpled now and then by a raindrop, stirred. The crying continued. How could she abuse *this* music? And the abundance of her tears distracted him. Could she produce this quantity on demand, or did the great flow come only after she lost control? Her clothes remained damp from the sleet.

"Darling, just stop thinking for a while. Just listen."

"But I can't! I can't do anything. I'm worthless. I'm nothing. I've tried to be good, my intention has always been to be good, to do good. I'm nothing. Oh, I don't *know* anymore. My life is over. I'll just go away, far away, where you won't have to bother about me ever again. Look at how Mother —"

He crouched over her, his arms and shoulders tense; at any moment sharp blows could fall. "She called — to tell you she's put her jewelry in her shoes. And to find out if you were coming. Do you want to go to her?"

"What?" She blew her nose. "How's *your* mother? I don't see you visiting your mother. You stuck her in a home and forgot about her."

He did not say that the home for his mother was Melpomene's idea. Only violence would result. Once again he fell silent, once again he allowed the world to be the way Melpomene made it.

She continued to sob. "What about me? I don't ask anything. I'll never ask anything again, not even a little comfort. Oh, you don't know how empty I feel. How alone I am."

"*Ruhet sanfte, ruhet wohl,*" sang the choir.

He stroked her back. (It reminded him of his grandmother's back!) She was so small-boned, so frail. He would die for her.

She cleared her throat, lifted her hand, and studied her thumb. "Of course I have to go to her — I told you that. I told you that last week. I told you several times. I distinctly remember on Tuesday —"

"No," he heard himself say. "No, you didn't." If he kept silent in the presence of one more of her lies, he might pitch forward, an infernal pain might lance his chest. He might lose himself forever. But the fear! Uncontrolled, what could she do to him? Anything. Never mind. "Stop it," he said. "I don't want to hear another lie from you. It hurts me. It hurts you. We said we wanted only the truth. You must have forgotten. I mean, you have the freedom, darling. Freedom is something we —"

She pulled away from him. "My God! You should hear yourself. I wish I had a tape recorder!" She made her voice high-pitched and foolish. " 'You have the freedom, darling.' " Her voice dropped and became grating. "You are *so* smug. You disgust me. You always think that you're in the right, that you're so good. I can't stand your so-called kindness. You're nothing. A goody-goody, a prim old maid. You don't care who you crush with your arrogant self-righteousness! You don't even see this wound on my thumb!"

Yes, she hated him. They were alone here, in this cold room in which no one ever set foot, in which the chairs and sofas faced away from each other. They were far from help — what help? — and he was ready to vomit from fear.

He struggled against the quaking in his voice. "You — you're, you must never speak to me that way again." She stared at him, opened her mouth, and then closed it.

He knelt on the hearth and piled twig upon twig. That first night, when her luminous face dominated the table, and the back of her head dissolved in darkness, and the city had roared up around the room where the dinner party was being carefully and correctly conducted, as if they were all actors, he had thought: she wears her mask tightly; she's exciting; she's too dangerous for me. But soon he had fallen into a sublime intoxication, and its waves and eddies washed over any inconsistencies. Stunned that a woman as beautiful, as bright and youthful and independent as Melpomene

had decided to exalt him, apt phrases poured from his mouth; in bed he performed like a satyr. She had transfigured him into a towering soul, strong, pure, important.

He shook his head, and on top of the twigs he placed bits of kindling. The first time she had screamed at him, he thought his heart would fail. He was still married then and had neglected to return her phone call promptly because his wife had been rushed to the hospital. Melpomene told him that he was rude and nasty. This thunderbolt silenced him altogether. All he had wanted at the end of that dreadful day was to lie in her arms (he had frantically gone through his wife's pill bottles searching for which ones she had emptied into her mouth so that he could inform the emergency room doctors; she had come home six weeks later with some pottery bowls she had made; and a few months after that, she scarcely protested when he brought up divorce). But Melpomene eventually forgave him, the terror ended, and, his cheek against her breast, he floated in an ocean of bliss; he would live forever.

Sleet ticked against the shingles. Startled flames sprang up and snapped at the twigs and branches. Before waking this morning, he had descended into a Botticelli glade, swum in Canaletto waters; her hair had spread on the pillow. If only he could regard her steadily, as a chiaroscuro, and hold the contradictory parts in his mind at once. "*Schlummern da die Augen ein. . . .*" The voices sang as purely as if they had been carved out of fresh, cool air.

Eleven

SHE LAY on a sofa with her hands over her face. Branches banged against the roof. Kuno knew how frightened she was of storms. But he didn't care. How could he write to her from Europe, call her from the air, even evoke Notre-Dame and their sacred union in front of the mirror (she twisted the gold ring from her finger and dropped it between the sofa cushions), and yet now that he was back not even want to see her or even answer her calls? Vanished, and he had been her god! More than God, since God had created a crazy world of agony, and all Kuno tried to do was paint.

At her funeral she would have the St. Matthew Passion played. She would leave a memorandum with someone she could trust — but who could she ever trust? Ruth? Ellen, perhaps — to make sure all her instructions were carried out exactly. The fire in the blurred windowpanes erupted in a dozen jumping shapes. Rows of mourners would sit in pews. The architect. The governor. The conductor. The

archaeologist. The poet who said he owed her all his inspiration. James, the insufferable suffering widower, with
Alice on his arm. Kuno in the back, a wraith. The long
black box would be heaped with lilies and a single light
would shine down from above. On her finger the little gold
ring. She no longer wanted to do anything.

You see? said a cracked and wicked voice. You see? The
heated alternation between yes and no had dried up the
waters of her life. Ruined her. She retrieved the ring and got
to her feet, a little dizzy.

The mirrors in the flickering light of the living room were
kind. You are a spirit, they said as she passed; a pilgrim soul
touched with the gold of the fire; you are not damned; you
are courageous. Not so the mirror in the powder room
where the rigid linen towels hung. Lit by three strong overhead lights, it was like the one the demons in the fairy
tale had made to cast back upon the angels the ugliest and
most deformed reflections of themselves. The demons had
laughed so hard as they were carrying the mirror up to
heaven that it shivered and broke into thousands of fragments that lodged in the eyes and hearts of mortals below.
Once she'd given a talk using "The Snow Queen" as her
text: the tears of caritas must wash away the distorting
shards. This bathroom mirror, no doubt a project of James's
first wife, had a supremely unflattering cant and made the
faces it received drawn, rucked, puffy. Old. What had the
world done to her? This hostile place, frozen and dark, and if
the sun came out it scorched and withered you. This planet
had to be a mistake. She washed her face again and again.
Her nerves stung. Never again would Kuno lie down by her
side and hold her and press his mouth to hers. Her one hope

had vanished. Being human was a terrible, terrible mistake. "Look what they've done to me," she whispered to the mirror woman, gaping with fear.

He prodded the fire and listened through the music to the running water in the powder room. His first wife had insisted on keeping that room just so, with little perfumed soaps, and a basket for discarded hand towels; she enjoyed having guests. Perhaps a party would help; Melpomene would glow, and hurry around, putting her friends at ease. It occurred to him with a start that he no longer had any friends of his own. How had that happened? She had shyly indicated to him the flaws of various men he knew; she had the intuition that they might steal his ideas. And from the beginning it was clear that she would not tolerate his women friends, no matter how platonic. "Aren't we complete company for each other?" she asked. "I love you so much more than all your friends put together." Even when she heard him speaking briefly with Ruth before passing the telephone to her, her face became grim.

But on occasions when the guests were her former lovers, or selected members of the fellowship, she was especially acute, laughing, gently joking, flirting. That was what had drawn him to her the night they met — that, and a feeling of fate. Her voice, when she was not distracted, was melodious and resonant. He loved to hear her read aloud. She had a light step; he always pictured a little girl when he heard her on the stairs. But the woman now emerging from the powder room had adopted a heavy, slow tread and dry, querulous speech. Self-pity (he had to say it) had stretched out her tones and robbed them of their fullness. Her habits had helped time ruin her beauty. How strong she must be to endure herself! He stabbed at a stripped cedar branch, and it fell apart into chunks of glowing blood-red, releasing the energy that had been stored over the springs and summers of the tree. Until today he had seen her only peripherally, a blink at a time. He had always quickly forgotten what he had just witnessed and, needing her lovely attention on his every syllable, he would promptly create another image to sustain himself.

He was about to ask her if she were ready for dinner when, head down, hand stretched out as if she were sleep-walking, she went into her study and slammed the door.

Under the house, the cold earth was waiting. The sleet was only sleet, and the earth was only earth. Nothing more.

The telephone rang in Kuno's apartment. His recorded voice offered a new greeting. "I have returned, *mes amis,* but it may be awhile before I can return your call. Please be patient." He had gone out to some sparkling party, or he lay in bed with another woman, and they would laugh at Mel-pomene, at how pathetic and inane she sounded. Please be patient! No one had been more patient. She held the receiver and did not speak.

She glanced up at the Pinocchio angel with its overly long nose and blank eyes. From now on she would be alone. She had appealed to him for help — something she had long ago vowed never to do — and, like all the others, he had failed her. If she were ever to have a lover again, he could come and go as he liked. She wouldn't care about him as long as he performed in bed. She would ask nothing else. (Oh, but you're old and ugly now; who are you to make such demands?) And her husband no longer mattered. How dare he give her orders on how she should speak? He had been her revenge on Kuno, and had turned out to be nothing but a stumbling block, practically impotent, a big, dumb piece of furniture, an awkward breakfront that had looked good in the murk of the antiques shop, thanks to a bowl of wax fruit and a vase of silk flowers, but was all wrong for the house. No wonder she didn't want people to know about him.

From now on she would be alone. Completely orphaned and alone. Her mother — never a real mother; if anyone was the mother in that family, it had been Melpomene. In any case, one of these days she would finally kill herself or die. Hard to know how she really was, complaining, making gestures of farewell; she was a woman who could stage any emotion she liked. (Ah, we're just the same! Horrible thought, but true.) Maybe Melpomene ought to visit (no one lasts forever) even though it meant losing time when she had a talk to prepare and services on Sunday and committee meetings. No, Kuno, I can't be with you. Goodbye forever, James — you won't have to hear me speak ever again. She saw herself counseling her mother; urging her to be brave; tenderly bringing a cup of broth to the ancient lips; reading her inspirational quotations from the Bible, the Bhagavad Gita, the Metaphysical poets. Melpomene could give a talk about being at the side of a loved one, accompanying the beloved for the last time. *Or ever the silver cord be loosed, or the golden bowl be broken, or the pitcher broken at the fountain, or the wheel broken at the cistern. Then shall the dust return to the earth as it was; and the spirit shall return unto God who gave it. Vanity of vanities, saith the preacher; all is vanity.* But if the old woman were to continue these threats after the visit was over, then what? Bring her here to live, that was it; serve her, a penance, the good daughter at last.

And how was Melpomene going to get to her, to rescue her from hell? Because of Kuno, because of James, because of the predatory Alice, Melpomene was in no state to do anything, to go anywhere. It would be a miracle if she ever got up from her desk again. Her head throbbed. She had barely managed to shove her suitcase into the trunk, and the roads were bad, and Kuno, who could have driven her safely, would not answer his phone. If she couldn't reach her mother in time, then all of them were to blame. And her mother as well, for neglecting her, for lying to her over the years, for failing to love her.

James climbed the steps — the aroma of the simmering vegetables hung in the stairwell — and went into his study. He wanted to cry like a child, or a feeble old man. He was starving. His jaw hurt again. His knee ached more than ever, for no reason at all; his whole skeleton had awakened.

The girl, caught for a split second in the midst of a half turn, gazed down at him; all this time, she had not been beckoning him to an erotic adventure but rather telling him something much more important. To follow her. He now saw that her expression was divided: one eye was sad, because she knew he probably would not, and the other was adamant, commanding him to make the effort. Through a tremendous, sustained concentration, Mauritius had put his entire being and thought into that painting. Not one faltering brushstroke; not one point of light wrong in the blurred inexactitude of the boundary of flesh against the darkness.

James forgot Melpomene, he forgot his fear, his knee, his envy, his vanity. The girl was projected toward him with absolute clarity, a ray of coherence in the meaningless black chaos; she shimmered, real, immediate, breathless. The most familiar of scenes, in which you come upon a woman in a private moment and, surprised, she turns. The simplest reality is saturated with mystery and promise. James had felt limited in his ability to perceive painting and music, but he hadn't realized how distant he was from even one moment of his own life. Mauritius had breathed, had disappeared, leaving this record of all he knew about what it was to live. James, temporarily present, would soon disappear, but in this radiant moment, as long as eternity, his eyes were open, he was thinking for himself, and he was at last permitted to see, really to see, freed of the clutter of habits and assumptions and self-importance. An unreasoning joy billowed up.

He opened the desk drawer and felt in the back, behind the gun wrapped in the sock, for the velvet case. The gun. How stupid of him to hide the razors and forget the gun! But even though she would never go through his things (as he would never go through hers?), he had to find a better hiding place. Behind some books on the shelf. What books would she be least likely to take?

He sat down. He knew nothing about her. She might choose any book in preparing her talks. After dinner, when he wasn't so hungry, he would take the gun out to the garage and lock it up in a toolbox. But sometimes she used tools — suddenly he might find her with a crowbar, ripping out a wall. He could put it under the sacks of fertilizer in the garden shed, but one day he might look out and see her digging in the lawn. After she had moved in, one Saturday afternoon the grounds committee, along with other volunteers, had come and planted a thousand bulbs. As in a dream he had stared out the window at the yard he had known since infancy and, seeing it filled with smiling strangers with trowels, understood that he had no idea what he had taken on by marrying Melpomene.

The pearls. Pendant from their fine gold chain, they lay against velvet the color of a moonlit sky. For her birthday, in three more months. He would have preferred now to keep them for himself, but what use had he for pearls? Each one was a pale universe, softly gleaming, so sweetly liquid and cool in his palm, so elusive, that he wanted to hold them in his mouth.

Tonight he would give her the necklace. Tonight, because they had both grown old, because, for all her devotees and policeman callers and waifs and secret phone calls, she was alone. And he was alone. He would give her the pearls because he did not love her and because he did love her and because he was frightened and because she had once told him he was a virile genius and because he felt horribly sorry for her and because he understood now that pity meant the end of passion. Because the gaze of the girl said: Leave all you have and follow me. Because round white pebbles of ice lay on the windowsill.

Out in the drive, the sky pelted him. He opened the trunk of her car and lifted out the heavy suitcase and made for the door of her waiting room. Without knocking, he entered the study and found her bent over her desk — did she really have a dowager's hump now? impossible, but there it was — the phone receiver between her ear and her shoulder, her uptilted face in the mirror startled, her cheeks wet and shiny.

He put down the luggage, handed her the velvet case, and went out.

Kuno, dreaming of two bald, old men, twins, grinning at him, stirred; the bed was an immense sulphurous plain; he had done something wrong that could never be corrected. If he could wake up and answer the phone he would survive; but he couldn't move; he couldn't open his eyes. He and Melpomene, her head on his chest, floated in a bed like a shell above the clouds, blown by a storm.

"And the serpent said unto the woman, ye shall not surely die." The black lines wavered against the glaring white, tormenting her eyes.

If Kuno picked up the phone, she would say nothing. He might hear her sobbing. He'd have to apologize; she would wait. Or she would hang up. And never think of him again.

Her eye came to rest on a photo of herself in the embrace of a condemned man. One of the most beautiful faces she had ever seen. The Supreme Court refused to hear his case. She and other ministers had fought for him, and her name had been in the papers. She was convinced of his innocence, even a little in love with him, and he had declared his love for her, but there was nothing to be done. After a number of delays, the execution was scheduled.

"Are you afraid?" she had whispered. She had prepared herself with quotations and assurances, and she could feel the force of her unbending will. Yes, this was death. And she could help him. A beneficence flowed out of her like warm milk.

"No," he said. He seemed absent. He scarcely listened to

her. She wept on his shoulder and promised to be with him at the end.

Early in the morning she came, wearing a dark blue dress that hung in soft folds, to the unheated, whitewashed stone building where he was to be killed. She chose the bench closest to the chair. She wanted her face to be the last of this world he would look upon. She wondered if the bare bulbs overhead would dim. Would a hood be put over his head? What a horrible, suffocating thought! Not to breathe free air in your last moments, to subside in your own stale exhalations! But she had been told the current melted the eyeballs, and she didn't think she could witness the disappearance of his piercing, intelligent eyes. She made small talk with a reporter. She put her hand on his arm and sighed. "He's lucky. We're the ones who have to go on being afraid of death, not even knowing how long we have."

She had not slept in two days, the room was freezing, and the bench was hard. Finally, telling the reporter that she had reason to believe another stay had been granted, she got up and left. Later, she read in the paper about the execution and her anguish did not leave her for a long time.

Nothing ever left her, really. All the hideous deeds she had committed went on committing themselves, all the bad thoughts had long bodies, stretching over the years, all the wounds remained completely fresh, as did all the loves.

When the door opened and the wind blew in and the case was pressed into her unconsciously outstretched hand, she created in an instant a detailed event. Kuno, who relished a drama, had parked down the road and slipped into her waiting room. His plan was to stay in the dark, watching her phone him, and, just as she began to cry, he would enter the study and hand her the gift she had always wanted. Her pain assuaged, she would forgive him. That was the story that emanated from the brass lamp, the yellow light along the wall, the bust of the angel. When she saw the man's face in the mirror, and realized he was not Kuno, she didn't recognize him.

But it was only James. It was only his hand, and his familiar form, head down, graying, jowly, drops falling from his wet clothes onto the tree-of-life carpet. He went out, leaving her in her agony. Why was he handing her this box? Was it something of hers? A gift? Divorce papers? Their anniversary, and she had forgotten? She forgot so much these days — and her memory had once been the envy of everyone.

How could he do this to her? The antique necklace she had tried to buy for herself and had learned was sold. How had he known? She had wanted it, he'd seen her desire. She would be forced to be grateful. He had won. The pearls glowed creamily in the subdued light, disgusting — extravagant and disgusting. He must have paid a lot. He must have caught her looking at them that day in the antiques shop; he had intruded on her private moment the way he sometimes spied on her in the shower or in her closet when she was getting dressed or when he thought she was asleep. Seen her when she did not choose to be seen. He had the impertinence to think he knew her taste, and now he was exploiting his findings to humiliate her.

She would go away. The pearls, obviously offered out of fear, obviously bought for Alice, would be left behind on her desk. No, on his desk, the expensive desk she had given him, next to the gun. No note. Let him figure out the message. The pearls brimmed violently with some substance that was about to expand, to fill the room, to press her against her chair and suffocate her.

The fragrance of the bubbling pot, the steam printing shields on the windows, and beyond the warm, lit-up room, the darkness lanced by sleet, made him oddly happy. He himself was the bathing girl, the woman weighing gold, the canal scene, the wedding couple. He had only to look, and a thousand, ten thousand, universes opened up to him. His house held the treasures of the world. In the turbulent night sea were islands, and he now found himself on this particular one, floating in the black, viewing the dread that lapped the shore on all sides.

At least he had made his stand. Perhaps she would love the necklace, and everything would become new again. But he had seen that she hated accepting the case from him. He had to push it against her fingers before she would open them; he caught her sullen upward glance. She might love the pearls or she might dissolve them in vinegar, as Cleopatra had done to prove a point.

Melpomene had once explained to him that gifts rather than love had been the currency in her family, and she still felt injured every time she received a gift. Their first Christmas, then — he was still living with his wife — he did not give her any gifts to open. Rather, he planned to take her on a carriage ride and give her an elegant dinner at a hotel; no easy feat to escape from his wife on a holiday. But when he opened the present Melpomene had given him — a bronze candelabrum he was later to learn had been a farewell present from a previous fellowship — he noticed that she was ashen and silent; she disappeared into her bedroom. After several minutes he joined her. She lay on the bed and announced that she did not want to live. Why? The pain, she said. Not to have one gift on Christmas morning! But what about the bouquets and wreaths, and the piles of packages on the mantelpiece? Those were not from people who loved her; those had not arrived on Christmas day. "But I'm taking you to dinner, something very special," he said, coloring. "Is that a *real* present?" she asked, and began to cry. He hurried home and, when his wife was not looking, unlocked his safe. That was how Melpomene had come to receive his grandmother's canary diamond brooch, which she still had never worn.

He had given her pain when he gave her gifts and pain when he had not. Odd that he hadn't observed this confusion before but rather only inhabited it, blind, hurt, anxious for her life. He was slow, stumbling, as susceptible to her violent, unpredictable storms of affection as to those of her hatred. Standing in the kitchen, watching the carrots bob in the broth, he was struck by the uselessness of her facile theories and interpretations and beliefs. Baffling, since she spent her days helping people. Who knew what was true about her? Who knew why she did the things she did? Perhaps she simply acted. The sun shone. The wind blew. No reason. Later she would make up an explanation. Her story about her childhood as a sort of neglected prodigy might be one more invention. She may have been abundantly loved. He had heard her mother speak about Melpomene with pride and fondness.

He longed to sit his wife down across from him, take her hands, and say, Please tell me the truth. I want to know who you really are. What you really want. What would make you happy. Please. He toppled from his island, and the dread returned.

She dropped the pearls from one hand to the other. If she kept them, it would mean her surrender. He would then know that he had given her what she wanted. She would be the object of charity, indebted to him, dependent; drawn by his noose wherever he liked. Or did he think she was a prostitute, willing to be bought? But of course the necklace had been intended for Alice. That was indisputable. Why else would he have hidden it? And now, he somehow knew that she had found out about Alice and he was afraid; or he wanted to atone for his brutalities. When he had forced the velvet case on her, and she understood that the hand was his and not Kuno's, she knew she had been robbed.

The thin gold chain was finely worked; the clasp must be early Georgian. The pearls were perfectly matched. She could almost feel the presence of the woman who had originally worn them. She had a pink bosom, and was vain about it, and conducted a salon, and was paid homage by many lovers — poets, painters, composers, sculptors, architects, politicians.

What would a good person, a person of spiritual development, an evolved person, do? Christ understood that the people around Him were unwashed, crude sinners, that one of them would betray Him. But He forgave. (The angelic host had sung in the living room. The oak tree had flamed in the morning sun.) Perhaps Judas was the most important of all the disciples; without him, there would have been no crucifixion.

*

He had spread the linen that they used only when guests came, and set the dining table with his grandmother's goblets, china, and silver, and lit the candles in the bronze candelabrum. Very well, then, she would be the dutiful guest. It was his house. She would ask nothing.

They sat opposite each other. He drank cool wine from his goblet; he nearly wept when he tasted the soup. It was as if he had never eaten before. Melpomene had once told him about a meditation certain monks sometimes used at mealtime: to consider the source of every morsel. The vegetables had stored up their sweetness and pungency under the earth; animals had surrendered their being to produce the broth; all the nutrients needed for sustaining life had come from the soil, the water, and the sun. What had he done to merit this? Nothing. He had been born naked and ignorant. He had played more than he had worked. And yet all this energy and matter had been stirred together and dedicated to keeping him alive. He was being fed. "Do you remember that meditation the monks do at Athos, or wherever, when they eat? I was just —"

"Please don't humor me. You don't have to talk about what you think interests me."

(The cup and plate were broken. Under the floor lay the cold earth.)

"I just thought of it, that's all. How we take what we eat for granted. But think of all the work."

So obvious always! He was begging her to compliment his efforts to cook, and hoping she would say something about the pearls. She fingered them. Because he had seen her admire them and then bought them for Alice, Melpomene would wear them in cynical triumph. She would

also wear them when she met Kuno (certainly they would meet again), so that he would recognize that another man valued her highly enough to surround her with gifts more lavish than Kuno would ever be able to bring himself to give. She would come down a curving staircase into a room with dark red velvet curtains, and she would wear the white dress, and the pearls, and she would stand in the center of the room under — under a chandelier, yes — stand very straight, trembling a little, and he would see her and stare and swallow, as moved as a groom waiting at the altar when his bride appears at the end of the aisle.

James sat across from her, jaws working. She could hear him chewing his bread. She had no interest in food; her head ached. He spoke. His voice was always a little grating. He had been so ardent during their courtship — until she'd let him make love to her. Harsh and controlled, that's how he was tonight, even though she had made it obvious that she had forgiven him: she had put on the pearls and come to dinner when he called her, like an obedient dog. And even presented him with the rechargeable flashlight, a very wonderful gift! Didn't he notice her humility? Wasn't that enough? What threw him into such domineering moods? He should have had the courage to tell Melpomene about this Alice instead of sneaking around and writing such garbage.

"Just taste it," he was saying.

She toyed with her spoon.

"You'll feel better." He made his voice forceful. "Darling, eat!"

She touched her spoon to the rim of the bowl.

It was a very good soup. She could scarcely believe his

claim that it was all his own doing. When she met him, he hadn't known how to boil an egg. In any case, the meal was hot and surprisingly delicious.

Suppose some homeless wanderer in the storm came along. He would look through the bay window into the dining room. He would find two people enclosed in light, facing each other across a table; he might even deduce that she wore pearls of great price and that the glass of the goblets was thin. Suppose Kuno were to drive by: this is the tableau he would see. See and envy. How poorly he concealed his jealousy of James! When Kuno was still married (just after they fell in love) and she was the homeless wanderer, she sometimes would pass his place and watch him at the dining table with his wife.

Now she could think of Kuno only lying in a coffin. He had been stricken by a heart attack in the street; his car had crashed and burned on the highway as he sped toward her; no one would understand that she was the person who ought to be notified.

The phone in her study rang and she dashed from the table.

"Yes, Gabriel?" She made her voice musical. So he wanted to see her again!

Kristen had been pulled out of the bay. Someone had spotted a swimmer too far out at twilight, but by the time a boat reached her, she was gone. Was Melpomene needed? She could come immediately. No, the family had been called; her mother was on her way.

When Melpomene returned to the table, she wore an expression James had never seen before, traced with pain and yet serene; alert and reconciled. Steady. Was this her true face? Slowly, as if engaged in a private ceremony, she picked up her spoon. Staring at her, an inaccessible work of art, he felt sorrow: she was a mystery he would never know.

She lifted the empty spoon to her lips like an orphan child, the fingertips of her free hand touching her collarbone.

He might still be youthful enough to attract a lovely younger woman. Or perhaps he could find Alice again. How could she ever grow old? The bathing girl. Eternal. He often daydreamed about women, pivoting to watch them on the streets of the city or on the train platform or in the supermarket. In restaurants he peered around like a connoisseur in a gallery. But usually beautiful women were connected to other men, and tonight exhaustion prevented him from even daydreaming about a chase, let alone a conquest. And even if he were to begin an affair, or simply pick up a woman for the afternoon, his terror of Melpomene was so great that he would be paralyzed, even if she were on the other side of the world. He wished for rest. He would stop here, with Melpomene, and simply endure her.

Soon he and she would be too old to seek out lovers. The furtive telephone calls would be a matter for jokes. They would sit in the kitchen, stooped, half-blind, barely able to hear each other. He thought, Her mother is right — Melpomene is lucky to have me, and, for now, I'm lucky enough to have her.

For no good reason, for no gain she could discover, James, in his clumsy way, had tried to be kind to her, he had helped her, and she had paid little attention, no more than she did to the sun coming up every day. "James, I have something to say to you. I've behaved shamefully, horribly. Can you forgive me?"

"Of course."

As she considered his irrational goodness, and that he might die or disappear, tears came to her eyes, and she was forced to bow her head over the bowl of aromatic soup. And I forgive him, she announced to herself. Not in theory, but from my heart. And never again will I wrong him. Worthless, penitent, hopeful, she saw herself dissolving in the rain.

Twelve

HE PUT his arm around her and they climbed the stairs, bits of their passing forms daubing the panes of the stairwell window. A chill exhalation rose with the smell of earth from under the boards. Sleet hammered the house and tore the leaves from the trees.

They had entered this house temporarily. They lived the life of this house. They took on the work of this house. They repaired it and cleaned it and used it and broke its contents and repaired them and broke them again. They labored here and rested here. The mirrors and windows caught them and released them.

They thought about other things, about anything except what was happening to them, what was going to happen, when their skin met the air, when night fell, when, one foot on the threshold, they had to say goodbye.

*

They moved through the room in exactly the patterns they followed every night. The chest of drawers and the corner cupboard made their mute wooden presences known to the two upright human bodies. *We are just the same. You bravely come and go. We remain.* Lamplight blossomed in the mirror; a second lamp; the bathroom light. Three pools of illumination overlapped. The furniture, soft as shadow, eased back against the walls.

He brushed his teeth. Hadn't he just gotten out of bed and brushed them a few minutes ago? The day, his magnificent empire, had started out whole and then had shattered into smaller and smaller bits. He spat. He had trusted her more deeply than he had ever trusted anyone.

The light from the windows enclosed slanted chambers in the dark air filled with arrows of sleet. She washed her face and looked calmly in the mirror and at the flailing, nearly leafless oak beyond the window behind her head. The light here was forgiving; horrid details were blurred or erased. Otherwise she would have not looked at all at her face. Nevertheless, watching herself reaching for the maroon washcloth on its peg, she said to herself, I've grown old. I don't want to be alone. I will take myself in hand. And I will go to my mother — perhaps tomorrow.

He sat on the edge of the bed and felt the stubble on his jaw. All afternoon, shadows had been lengthening, as if that were their absolute right, as if the house, the lawn, and the woods were their domain, not his. Without his invitation, despite whatever he thought, the shadows lengthened. The darkness fell. The day was his and it was not his. This body was his and was not his. He did everything and he did nothing. He could conceive of permanence but he was temporary. He was only the witness. And he too was spreading and growing weaker, and his edges would eventually disappear into the darkness. But that couldn't possibly happen because he could sense his hand on his skin, he was alive, he had made a beginning today, he had at last truly seen a painting, he had become the music, he would go on. He could even make a plan for next week, next month, next — "Darling, what about a trip to — to northern Italy? Tuscany. Umbria. The Alto Adige." He loved saying those names. "Next spring, maybe?"

Toothbrush in her mouth, she gave a short ironic laugh. He would never, never understand. If she stopped for a minute, the world would stop. "Fully booked," she said.

"What? Drop all that for a bit. We can afford it. Let's live it up while . . ."

Silence, running water. He fell back on the bed and stretched. The sleet pitted the panes. Is it possible, he asked the bedroom ceiling, which was divided into zones of light and shadow, is it possible that I am going to die without learning anything about my life, about who I am and what I need to do? Is it possible that all these difficulties — the knee, the jaw, her sobs — are for nothing? Just particles in a fleeting configuration? I feel all right. A little tired sometimes. After a day like today, completely used up. Perhaps it's a good thing that she keeps herself so busy and so overwrought: she doesn't notice the emptiness.

He pulled the covers up to his chin. Tomorrow. Tomorrow he would continue. Tomorrow he would be better. The game would absorb him fully; the others would play their roles; no one would go inside when summoned. When he closed his eyes, the painting returned; the girl gazed at him, her lips parted. We remain. Tomorrow he would face his real work, the work he was put on this earth to do.

As she got into bed, she touched James's neck with her cold, damp fingers. I want to live in perfection. But I destroy each day as I live it, and I watch myself doing so. I wake up mornings happy and soon I'm miserable. A prisoner.

Now Kristen lay with water in her lungs and nostrils. Melpomene had imagined she could save her. Kristen had never done anyone any harm. What had she said this morning? Why do things have to change? When was Melpomene going to find the time to write the eulogy? She had scarcely started on her Sunday talk. Better not to think about Kristen. About the obscure intuition that had hovered over Melpomene during the day. She didn't make the call for Kristen; instead she went crazy; she forgot. Oh, God. But perhaps that was Kristen's destiny, and no matter what Melpomene might have done she couldn't have prevented it. And when she told James, he had agreed.

She picked up the book she was reading. *The Private Journal of Henri Frédéric Amiel.* "February 14, 1881. — Supposing that my weeks are numbered, what duties still remain to me to fulfill, that I may leave all in order? I must give every one his due; justice, prudence, kindness must be satisfied; the last memories must be sweet ones. Try to forget nothing useful, nor anybody who has a claim upon thee!" Only a few pages left to go. When she read, she could obliterate everything else. But she could not will her mind tonight to enter those words; she could not skip away down the sentences into a story that was not her own story, that was anybody's story, anybody's court case except her own, her very tiresome own.

They would say she was negligent. She would defend herself. Act as her own attorney, foil the prosecution, struggle with all her might against the death sentence, and win. No, they would not put the hood over her head. James and his judgments would not conquer her, nor would his kindness, which could level the airiest of spires. She would call Kuno. Tell him about Kristen. (She had tried to help Kristen — more than anyone else. She had meant to make the call. Oh, God! But there was no hope; nothing could have stopped her; the broken cup — that was how it was; things just got smashed; suicide was a hostile act.) Tell him about the importance of living consciously. A cautionary tale. Change him. He had to see that she was the best woman for him and that he was the best man for her. She would save him. And James as well. Kristen may have been the wise one in her ultimate choice. The bay, Kristen had drowned herself in the horrible bay, her pretty face would be bloated in the coffin. Didn't she once say that neither she nor Gabriel had ever recovered from their failure to love, to stay together? Oh, dear God, if You exist, forgive me! I ought to have held her, ought to have known, asked her to stay. I ought to have called her, swum out and rescued her. . . . The Sunday talk, think about that. . . . The garden, the tree, the fruit. . . . What was the garden? Not a place. . . . Blessed are they that do His commandments (I will never blindly obey any commandment, even from God; what kind of a God would take Kristen's life?) . . . that do His commandments

197

that they may have the right to the tree of life, and may enter in through the gates . . . (atoms began to break off from the substance of her mind and to float about in the room).

Tomorrow she would call Kuno and straighten him out. And she would have a long talk with James. What was bothering these men? But really, she thought, sinking and sinking, who are they? We arrive, we don't know how we got here. If we came from elsewhere, we can't remember. We can't even think about anything outside of space and time. Time is a substance — was that what Kristen said? Perhaps noise and crowds, colored lights, a string being plucked, a band tuning up. . . . We enter a house we suppose to be our own, but little in it is familiar; mysteriously, it keeps operating. A child appears — a stranger; perhaps there's some order to be made of all this, perhaps the rooms crammed with things we don't remember accumulating can somehow be organized. But everything keeps changing; first we're small, then we're big; then we're tired and fall asleep in unfamiliar places. Those we love show us their wounds; they find others to love; a shadow appears on a lung; we love someone and will never tell him; we've used up our energy on — we can't remember what, or how — oh, on petty things. . . . On what had she spent herself? . . . What seemed real had disappeared. What seemed unreal, what was waiting for her all along, calling to her, turned out to be very strange, obeying its own laws. She would put the book down for a moment and rest her head on the pillow, and pull the quilt under her chin, and wait.

A certain number of days were preserved in a row of clear glass spheres through which the sunlight easily passed and

on which reflections played. On those days, she did everything well, with intention. She woke up happy for no reason
at all. In good health. She did not brood. The doings of
others did not disturb her. She loved James and she loved
Kuno, and she loved all the others as abundantly as ever. . . .
Delicately attuned, she listened to the stories of the people
who sought comfort and help from her. She delivered her
talks with authority and kindness. She performed christen-
ings and weddings. She drank her milk and ate the muffin
James brought to her on a tray. They would weed the garden, or walk through the woods, or along the shore. In the
evenings, she read or worked on her talks. Perhaps at dinner
she and James would have a spirited conversation about art,
or about the nature of time, or evolution. In bed she would
become absorbed in a book. James, propped against pillows
under his own lamp, might read her a passage from one of
his Greeks. In the muted light the mirror looked kindly
upon her: Yes, you are still a beauty, a Georges de La Tour
Magdalene. She would fall asleep, awaken, read the same
sentence, and then fall asleep again. She might be reading
something useful and wise — about the transitoriness of the
moment and the task of truth and beauty and perfection,
about keeping close to duty when hope seems lost. In the
glass sphere, in the perfectly conscious day, added to the
string of transparent beads, she would give up the book and
the light at last and drop her head on the pillow, each of the
thousand moments completed calmly and well.

He lay still, listening. The wind and the sleet had ceased.
Her even breathing began to disintegrate the dark room.
The bonds between the bureau and the corner cupboard
dissolved, between the bed and the floor, between his body

and the mattress. . . . And his own breathing, his chest rising and falling, blotted out the mirror and the windows. . . . The precious cup, the plate, broken. One day the weather is serene; the next, a hurricane destroys the town. One day we are well, the next mortally ill. Life does all it can to bring us into being, then all it can to destroy us. We're still alive, she and I. Still alive. Warm waves surged toward him, and light played on the waves. He was lifted up. He would go — a long voyage — and he wanted to reach for her, to take her with him, but he could not make his hands move. The room disappeared.